BEING SUPER

HOW TO BE SUPER THROUGH TURBULENT TIMES

C. SMALLWOOD

First Edition: August 2020
Printed in the United States of America

ISBN: 978-1-7357330-0-5

TO ALL THE HEROES THAT HAVE INSPIRED ME
TO BE BETTER, AND ALL MY FRIENDS WHO
KEEP ME ON TRACK TO DO BETTER, AND MY
BRAVE & BOLD TEAM-UPS,
YOU ARE ALL SUPER TO ME!

Table of Contents

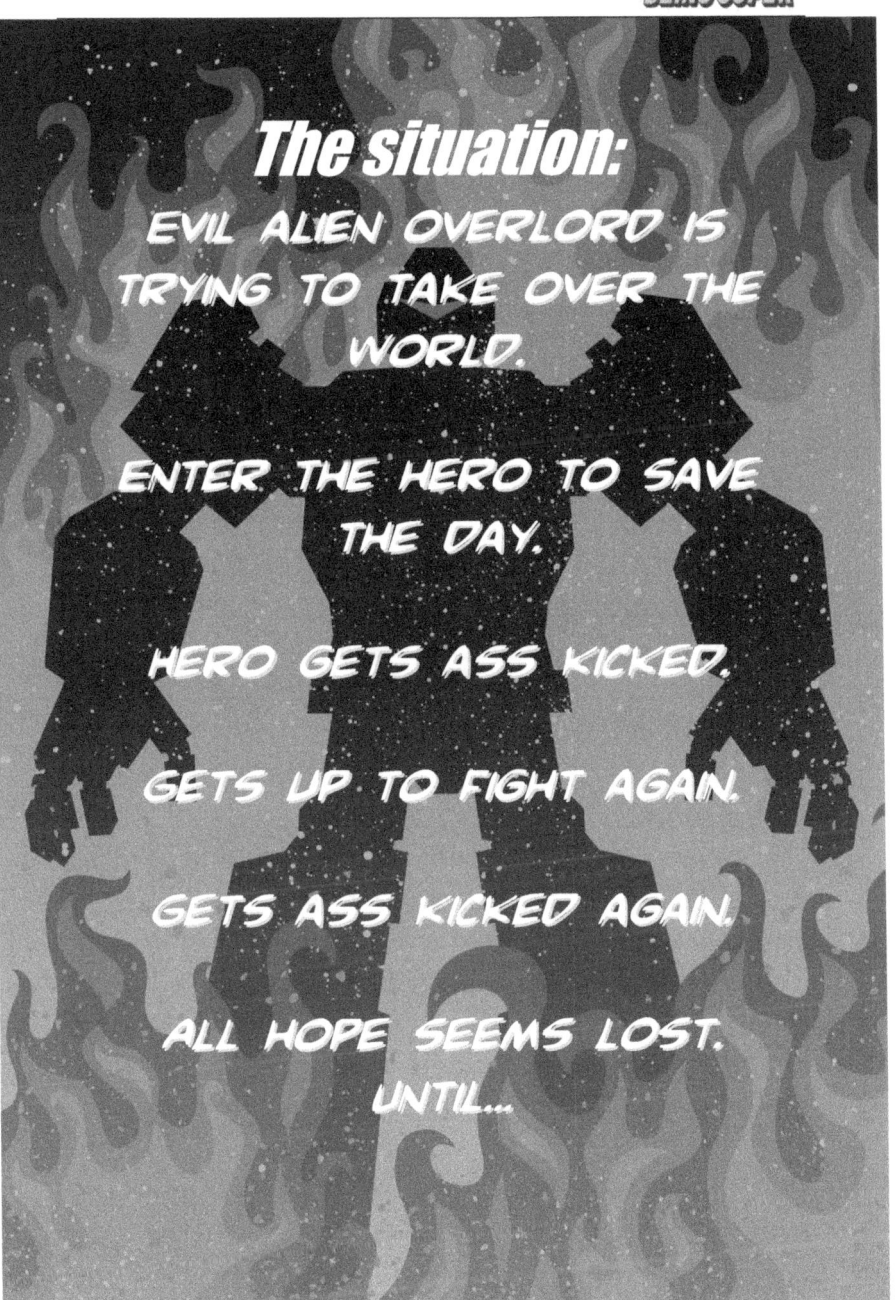

The situation:

EVIL ALIEN OVERLORD IS
TRYING TO TAKE OVER THE
WORLD.

ENTER THE HERO TO SAVE
THE DAY.

HERO GETS ASS KICKED.

GETS UP TO FIGHT AGAIN.

GETS ASS KICKED AGAIN.

ALL HOPE SEEMS LOST.
UNTIL...

⭐ INTRODUCTION

You've picked up this book and already are wondering, "Is this just about superheroes or is it something halfway useful?" The answer to both of those questions is a resounding, "It's so much more!"

You're familiar with superheroes. They are everywhere these days. You may be a fan and have a favorite, you may not. Either way, you don't have to be a super fan to understand the concepts and use the tools in this book to help you BE more to accomplish more.

This **BEING SUPER** book has been a labor of love for me the past 10 years. Well, more than that. Every time I would begin to write, an event would take place that required me to become a little more "super" for and would pull me away from writing. An event like a divorce, losing a job, death of close friends, loss of a business, a health issue. At the same time, every event would give me more understanding of what **Being Super** is all about and how it helped change my life.

This is a big deal for me. Tapping into the inspiration that is the hero story is what has gotten me through all the difficult times in my life. What I've been able to apply to my own life by learning from those heroes has been priceless: I've designed the life I want to live and can tap into my "inner hero" to accomplish all sorts of things. I want to share what I've learned with you so you, too, can tap into your "inner hero."

THE PLOT

Being Super is about how to stay true to yourself while engaging your inner hero and accomplishing your "big thing." It helps you stay strong and focused during turbulent times. That's why the title reads "Being." Not "been." Not "going to be." But "Being." Each day you make hundreds of decisions. Most are decisions made from habit, then others are decisions that can change the whole day's outcome. Depending on the day, your decisions can take you closer or further away from where you want to be in life.

Let's take a look at the journey of defining moments of a hero in a story, or as Joseph Campbell (an American mythologist, writer and lecturer, best known for his work in comparative mythology and comparative religion) called it, the Stages of the Monomyth. Campbell had 12 Stages the hero goes through on the journey. To simplify, I've broken it down to five pinnacle stages.

The Call

Before an adventure begins for every hero there is a sense of normalcy. Looking from the outside, we get a view into the everyday routine of life for the hero.

There's a level of contentment to the day-in-day-out activities. Everything is as expected in his world. The hero feels certain that tomorrow will be similar to today. The status quo is known to the hero.

It's your comfort zone.

In a flash of seconds, something happens to disrupt your calm. A fire breaks out, a burglar breaks in, the test results came back positive for cancer, you get a promotion, a drunk driver veers into your lane, you start a new business, a loved one suddenly dies, it could be anything. This moment thrusts you into a realm of unknowns. A new adventure. New territories to discover. No more comfort zone. Your world will never be the same.

You, the hero, start to feel the pressure. The

weight of responsibility. The deep-seated connection to protect and serve those around you. You discover there's more to your world than you thought. You realize you have a purpose. You get "the Call" to something greater, and you have to make a decision - to stay where you are or go on the quest.

The Quest

The adventure begins. A new quest has been laid before you. You know you're going to take down the villain and save the world, but don't know how to get there. Along the way, a mentor appears to teach you what you need to know for this quest. To point you in the right direction as a guide. To keep you focused. To help you overcome those first challenges. To help you not give up when the battle begins.

The quest is also the part of the journey where you discover what you are capable of. Strengths are discovered, weaknesses are overcome, tools are sharpened, and your core is defined. You're going to feel the change, and not always in your muscles. Your emotions will be heightened, your will tested. Your confidence formed.

Do you have what it takes to enter the battlefield?

The Battle

The time has come. The hero is face-to-face with the giant. This is the culmination of those decision moments along the quest. What will happen?

Invariably, you take a beating. It's the first time facing this foe. The villain was more prepared than you. So, you step back, analyze, regroup, form the plan, dig deeper, and take a deep breath.

This is the **defining** moment. Have you developed your super self to conquer the giant in front of you?

The moment seems bleak. Until you remember everything you've been fighting for along the way.

The importance of the mission. The impact this moment will have on your world. Take a deep breath, scream your battle cry, and advance into the fray.

The Victory

Standing amid the destruction caused by the battle, the hero stands victorious. The battle is won. Let the celebration begin! Time to recover. Time to sift through the ashes to see what remains.

The Continuing Adventures

The hero finds only remnants of his former self have survived. He has changed into something stronger. He is a new super-being. He is no longer able to return to the status quo. He knows his purpose. And he will live out that purpose to make his world a better place. Always vigilant. Always open and willing for a new quest. Always Being Super.

THE HERO

YOU are the hero. Think about it for a moment. You are the hero of your own epic story.

When do you KNOW you're a hero? Usually, it

comes well after the final battle that defeats the giant. And even then, there's barely a respite before heading into another battle. Sound familiar? As the old saying goes, "You are either coming out of a battle, going into one, or you are in a battle right now." And sometimes, it's all at once with different areas of our lives.

Heroes of old - the myths, folklore, and even the comic book superheroes of today, have a journey to travel. Some are seasoned heroes and others become the hero along the way. Some were eager for the adventure, others were hesitant to step into the role, and some accidentally fell into it (or got bit by it). But each hero story follows the same outline.

If you knew how the story was laid out, could you be more intentional about engaging your inner hero to make the best decisions to defeat your giants, win the battles, and create the life you want? Umm, yes.

Where are you in your journey?

THE BACKSTORY

Every good story has a back story to fill in the missing details on the hero. Here's part of my own back story and the journey to *Being Super*.

I grew up an only child in the middle of a rural area where my closest friends were the cows in the field near the house and dogs on the porch. I did not grow up in an environment that was fluffy and rosy. I grew up knowing that hard work equated to long days, dirty hands and getting results through the sweat of a brow, that figuring it out for yourself was the best way to learn, and that no one is going to do it for you. I grew up within a family that didn't know how to dream big, or didn't allow themselves to dream big. My mother became a mother very young and worked her butt off to provide for us. My dad was absent from my life. I had a LOT of alone time. So, in that alone time, I imagined a world for myself with the help of Saturday morning and after-school cartoons. Namely, Superfriends, Batman, Spiderman, He-man & She-Ra, G.I. Joe, Jem, Thundercats, Transformers, and the X-Men. Notice the theme? All heroes. Yes, even Jem was a hero - a ROCKIN' hero!

With the help of these heroes and their

adventures, I developed a mindset that made me want to make a huge positive impact in the world. Fast forward a bunch of years and a lot of life detours later, those superheroes and the inspiration they instilled in me long ago are still true today. In fact, over the years I've been blessed to observe a lot of other real-world heroes. Those people in all walks of life who go against the grain, head-on into battle, with a fire in their eye and purpose in their heart. Some do it instinctively, some have had training, and others didn't know they had it in them until the occasion called for them to be heroic.

I have had those heroes as personal friends and mentors who helped guide me to BE more during my darkest days and cheer me on to win the next battle. I hope to do the same for you with this book.

When I started writing **Being Super**, I was excited and overwhelmed with thoughts of what to include, how to arrange it, how to make it relevant, and write it in such a way that you would WANT to read it. Then stuff happens to get in the way of making time to sit and put my thoughts to the written word. Stuff I'm sure you have never been through:

- *Family drama*
- *Financial trials*
- *Feelings of betrayal*

- *Change of residence*
- *Loss of loved ones*
- *Relationship challenges*
- *Being abandoned by friends*
- *Health issues*
- *Times of depression*
- *Technical difficulties*
- *Identity crisis*
- *Moments when the world just crashes in on you all at once...*

Oh wait, that's right. You're human, too! You've had these things happen just like me.

While I was growing up I wanted to have **ADVENTURES**. I've always wanted to be the person that creates and accomplishes something so unique and great that it changes the world. Like Mother Teresa loving the lepers, Nelson Mandela changing a culture, Steve Jobs leading the movement to mesh creativity with technology, Zig Ziglar motivating the masses to "take it to the top," Condoleeza Rice helping women in the U.S. change the face of modern politics, Stan Lee creating heroes to thrill and inspire generations, Melinda Gates giving billions of dollars to philanthropy efforts, even Queen Elizabeth II who has stood as a pillar of strength, grace, and wisdom through an amazing amount of traumatic events over decades of history. The list goes on and on. I still want to be like them – the world changers. What I've come to realize is that I am a world changer - by changing the world around me. Start where I am - with me. Those small changes have a ripple effect on other people's "worlds." And one day, it can have an effect across the entire world.

I promise, this book is not about me and my accomplishments. Although, I will share what I believe are some of my favorite adventures. What I really want to give you are stories to inspire you, tools you can use to discover and strengthen your inner hero, and methods to stay on track to winning your own adventurous battles.

Let's get started...

 # THE CALL

IT WAS A BEAUTIFUL, SUNNY DAY. THE KIND OF DAY WITH A BLUE SKY CONTRASTING WITH THE GREEN LEAVES ON THE TREES AND DOTS OF WHITE PUFFY CLOUDS LOOK LIKE COTTON CANDY. IT WAS THE KIND OF DAY THAT MADE THE MUNDANE MAGICAL. THE SCHEDULE FOR THE DAY WAS ROUTINE AND THERE WERE NO EXPECTED CHANGES. STATUS QUO FELT GOOD. EVEN THE BIRDS SANG FAMILIAR TUNES. THEN IT WAS TIME TO DO CHORES AND ALL OF A SUDDEN - THERE'S A LOUD SOUND IN THE DISTANCE. SOMETHING HITS THE WATER CAUSING THE WAVES TO CRASH ONTO THE SHORE.

When you see someone who is successful, do you find yourself wondering, "What got them there?" It wasn't overnight that they became a genius-billionaire-philanthropist. So, what's their origin story?

Each of us has an origin story, not just the superheroes. Every decision, every circumstance, every conversation with others, and ourselves, everything we've learned and been through got us to where we are today.

The origin story begins with the Call.

CHAPTER 1
COMFORT ZONES

"WE COME INTO THE WORLD ALONE AND WE LEAVE THE SAME WAY. THE TIME WE SPEND IN BETWEEN - TIME SPENT ALIVE, SHARING, LEARNING TOGETHER - IS ALL THAT MAKES LIFE WORTH LIVING."

~Phoenix (Jean Grey)
Uncanny X-Men Vol 1 #303

THE COMFORT ZONE

Wonder Woman is my all-time favorite superhero. Many people know the 1970s TV version starring Lynda Carter who perfected the iconic image. However, Wonder Woman's stories have been going strong for over 75 years There have been a few re-starts to her storyline, but they all began with her comfort zone - living on Themyscira (Paradise Island), with only women, surrounded by her mother, the Queen, and Amazon sisters training daily to live the Amazon life of peace while studying the arts and the art of war. Until one fateful day, a man crash-lands on the island! Thus, the end of the comfort zone of Paradise Island and the beginning of a new adventure for Wonder Woman.

Every hero story begins with a safe zone aka the status quo. It offers a sense of surety and normalcy in a chaotic world. Every hero has a different version of normal. Some are farmers in the field and enjoy bright blue skies and soft winds. Others are the leaders of mega corporations doing business, and still others who come into the workplace and do their routine day after day. Then there are those whose normal looks like a battlefield of strewn legos, crayons, and juice boxes.

Comfort zones are a funny thing. They're like living in a child's playpen. You know the boundaries are there to keep you safe. All the things that make you happy surround you - food, drink, toys, entertainment. The support system is close by when you need company or something you can't do for yourself. A comfort zone keeps you comfortable. But, as a child grows out of a playpen, we should also be growing out of our comfort zone.

The fear of losing what secures us in the comfort zone is what can keep us there.

One of my favorite hero stories is in the Bible's book of Judges. It is about a man whose family and people have been overrun by the enemy for so long that he took to threshing wheat in a wine press. What makes this significant is that to thresh wheat you need to be in a wide-open space with some wind to separate the wheat from the chaff. Being in the winepress, Gideon was hiding from the enemy. That was his safe space. When out of the blue an angel of the Lord appears and says, "The Lord is with you, you mighty man of valor!"

Now come on. Mighty man of valor? Hiding in the winepress?

The angel goes on to call Gideon to save the Israelites from their enemy, the Midianites. Gideon, after questioning the situation and even making God show him that He really was talking to him, answers the Call and leaves his comfort zone to be used by God to lead the victory over the enemy.

In my own life, I have tiptoed over my comfort zone, taken giant leaps past it, and have been pushed forcefully beyond it in various ways and through lots of adversity. Not always because I WANTED to, but because it was necessary for me to grow beyond the person I was before the challenge:

- Childhood
- College
- Marriage
- Divorce
- Ministry
- College again
- Traveling internationally
- Getting fired
- Starting a business
- Ending a business partnership
- Losing decades-long friendships
- Seasons of bad health

- Restarting my life about a hundred times now...

From birth, I have been in a constant state of being pushed out of my comfort zone. Seriously. The push that began to define my adulthood didn't go well - it hurt a lot. I went from a tiny rural environment to a large university with zero knowledge of how to manage life on a college campus. It was overwhelming. I didn't know what to do and didn't know how to ask for help. I couldn't handle it and failed miserably. I went back home to what I knew and what I was comfortable with and did what was expected of me. I got a job and gave up on a dream.

I filled my life with other activities like teaching marching band and working extra jobs. But I was still on the path of what was expected. I even got married because that was the thing to do and would grow me into a new level of a person. I was right on that one, but not in the way I wanted. I had to grow into something new or be destroyed. I decided to grow into someone new.

This isn't just my story. I have many friends and colleagues who experienced a push out of their comfort zone in their lives. One couple's daughter began having seizures at 6 months of age and was told she wouldn't live past 2 years. Another friend's husband was diagnosed with brain cancer. A client of mine's husband had a stroke that debilitated him and caused her business, her life's work, to be on the brink of bankruptcy and closure. Yet another friend decided to start their own business and leave the corporate life. And another decided to follow her life's passion to be an artist, no longer a data entry person.

While all of this is happening, I'm reminded that Wonder Woman's comfort zone was thousands of years of island life focused on perfecting the ways of the warrior so she would be ready to leap into battle when it arose. That day came when Steve Trevor crash-landed on the island and she won the title of Wonder Woman to take him back to "Man's World." Once out of her peaceful world, she came face-to-face with the harsh realities of how power corrupts, and the powerless are defenseless. It affected her emotionally in ways she was not prepared for and she realized she was far from her comfort zone.

Whether we are pushed out of our comfort zones or we choose to leave, adversity and challenges happen. So do joy and happiness.

Once I realized and understood how adversity gives me the opportunity to grow and expand my comfort zone, I was able to tap into my inner strength and found faith in a higher power. I created a support system. And, I got some training. Every attempt afterward, to grow out of my comfort zone, has been an adventure that I am excited to take on. Because I know it levels me up, it doesn't tear me down.

What about you? Take a look around you now. What is your comfort zone? Your job, your lifestyle, your conversations, your income level, your health status? What is it that keeps you comfortable?

CHAPTER 2
DESTINY CALLING

"THERE ARE PARTS OF THE BOOK OF IRON FIST THAT ARE UNWRITTEN. AND RIGHT NOW, I AM THE ONLY GUY WITH THE PEN."

~Danny Rand

In the 2017 movie, Wonder Woman, Princess Diana knows her destiny is to defeat Ares, the God of War. This destiny, this definiteness of purpose, is what drives her throughout the story. She feels she was born for this. Everything she does revolves around moving forward to accomplish her mission. Nothing sways her, no one stops her - not even the German army in front of her as she crosses the No Man's Land battlefield. She is a force of nature. Her passion for her mission inspires others to join her in her quest.

Destiny can be a tricky conversation. The whole idea of destiny is believing that your life is meant for you to do something special, there's a purpose for everything, and the path you are on will lead you to it.

The thing is...not very many people believe in destiny, let alone that they have one.

Iron Fist is a Marvel character created by Stan Lee. The recent adaptation follows Danny Rand, the son of energy industry moguls, who was trained by mystical monks after finding him alive from a plane crash in the Himalayans that took his parents' lives. He believed that he had the destiny to defeat The Hand, an organization bent on destroying everything the monks held dear. Danny believed he could become the Iron Fist, protector of Kunlun. To become the Iron Fist, there were a series of trials ending in a battle to defeat the dragon that would grant him his Iron Fist Powers.

Once Danny has his powers, he returns to New York where the Hand organization has committed many nefarious deeds and he quickly gets to work on taking out the bad guys. Danny's focus is his destiny to destroy the Hand. Every decision he makes will lead him to his destiny.

If you knew your destiny, would you stay 'Iron Fist' focused?

In Napoleon Hill's book, Think and Grow Rich, he labels this kind of focus as "definiteness of purpose." The first step to accomplishing what we want is to have a burning desire so white-hot that it becomes definite and purposeful.

What do you have a burning desire for?

To have children? To have a career? To travel the world? To start a non-profit? To create a peaceful life? To pay the bills?

Or are you a blank slate?

Don't fret. Most people are trying to discover and define what they really want in life. Heroes don't always begin their stories with knowing their destiny. Sometimes, they are chosen by someone greater than themselves to fulfill a purpose they weren't aware existed. Sometimes it's a spiritual guide that sets us on the path. Sometimes it's our best friend.

Johnny Georges is a third-generation farmer in southwest Florida. He has maintained hundreds of acres of orange groves for decades with his family. In 1984, his father invented a more efficient way to water the trees. The "Tree Teepee" saved thousands of gallons of water while adding shelter for the trees during a frost. The reduction in water usage, and sheltering, meant that orange grove farmers could have crops during a frost or drought. This resulted in farmers being able to save trees and crops that ensured they would have revenue.

Johnny's best friend knew the potential of that invention. In 2013, unbeknownst to Johnny, he submitted Johnny's information to the television show, Shark Tank. To Johnny's surprise, he was accepted as a presenter to the Shark Tank panel. He appeared on the show with his dad's invention, the Tree Teepee. The episode itself is a reflection of this whole book's purpose mashed into an 8-minute segment. The result for Johnny was a victory that set him and his Shark Investor, John Paul deJoria, on to new and amazing adventures all over the world.

Johnny didn't ask for the opportunity and the whirlwind that came with securing a deal, but he quickly acknowledged his purpose in it: to honor his dad and do good for the farmers of the world.

I believe I have a destiny. Writing this book is part of that destiny. I have an insatiable desire for my life to have meaning and purpose. That desire gets energized every time I can provide help and value to someone else. Each time I fulfill a "definiteness of purpose" moment as part of my strategic plan I am fueling my overall destiny.

Destiny can be a tricky thing. When we use the perspective of definiteness of purpose, we can feel more in control of the direction we want our life to take. It is as if we had our own Iron Fist power.

CHAPTER 3
IT'S A CHOICE

"NO MATTER WHERE YOU TURN THERE'S A DECISION TO BE MADE. LIFE OR DEATH. RIGHT OR WRONG. REGULAR OR CRUNCHY."

~Frank Castle, The Punisher

Baby Kal-El was rocketed into space to arrive on Earth. When he was found by Johnathan and Martha Kent, they knew this child was destined for something world-changing. Kal, now called Clark, grew into his powers over time. As he grew into a young adult, he had a choice to make: use his powers to help the world or hide on the farm. He made a choice and Superman continues to be a symbol of hope for the world.

We are faced with hundreds of choices every day. Everything from what to wear and what to eat for dinner to who we want to partner with in life and which life insurance policy to choose. There are times when we feel like we have control over our choices, other times not so much.

I am fully convinced we are created beings made in three parts: Mind, Body, Spirit. The Spirit taps into the universal energy that surrounds us. The Body is obvious. It craves physical pleasure and needs to avoid pain. Thus, my desire for toes in the waves on the beach, rides on roller coasters, and the occasional bourbon. Then we have our Mind. And that is where our personal power truly lives.

Our mind is where we make decisions. It's where we think things through, remember and review, and sometimes over-analyze to the point of decision paralysis. Our mind is where we choose how we live in the world around us and relate with others. We choose the big things like job changes and where we will live, and the minor day-to-day things like what we watch on TV tonight. We create belief sets, preferences, and opinions with our mind. We choose to close off the world or welcome the world in. We choose to step-up or sit on the sidelines.

Steve Rogers chose to step up.

Steve Rogers was a scrawny, scrappy, frail young man from Brooklyn whose goal in life was to join the army to fight for his country. Because of his asthma, anemia, and short stature, Rogers was denied admittance multiple times. The Call came for Rogers one day when an Army scientist observed him and approved him as a candidate for the Super Soldier program. Rogers quickly stepped up and was injected with a secret serum that transformed him into Captain America, a tall, muscular, agile, and super strong man Steve Rogers' choice to step into a risky program that could potentially cause death, but could help him become bigger and stronger as a man to help the war effort, changed the world. The inspiration of

Captain America continues to change the world through comics, movies, and novels today.

When I lost my corporate job in 2009, I was faced with a major decision: to get a job, or to create a new life with a business of my own. Up until that moment, I had lived my life as expected - get a job with benefits including a 401K and two weeks of vacation, live within a budget, behave, and just get by. The other option was filled with risk and adversity and unknowns. And, seriously out of my comfort zone. But, I felt called to it. So, I chose the hard way. Needless to say, it has been an adventure. Losing that job really did give me an opportunity to do something different with my life.

Nowadays, when I have choices to make, I take a moment to see what's going on and how it fits with my destiny. If the options align with the direction I am going, I say "Yes." If it doesn't, it's not an option.

I had a choice whether or not to even write this book. What the heck do I really know about being a hero? I'm not like some of my friends who have willingly signed up and served in the military. Or other friends who knew from a young age they wanted to be a firefighter or police officer - the "run into danger" type. Or even like some of my friends who are nurses and doctors that fight unseen deadly villains every day. I would be remiss if I didn't mention all my teacher friends who deal with all those kids. They are obviously heroes.

What I have discovered while preparing for this book is that the superhero traits I admire in fictional characters are also found in real life examples all around me. So why not look inside myself as well? Do I have what it takes to complete the Call? (You're reading this book, that answers the question with a resounding YES).

When the Call comes, what do you choose? To step up and accept the adventure of a quest? Or to sit down and let the circumstances surrounding the Call event decide for you?

 # THE QUEST

WITH A DEEP BREATH AND SHAKY HANDS, HE GRABS HIS BAG AND HEADS INTO THE UNKNOWN. THE ADVENTURE BEGINS FOR THE HERO, A NEW QUEST HAS BEEN LAID BEFORE HIM.

HE PONDERS WHETHER HE'S READY, DOES HE HAVE WHAT IT TAKES TO ACCOMPLISH ALL THAT IS PUT BEFORE HIM?

WITH THE SAFETY OF THE WORLD ON THE LINE AND BUTTERFLIES IN HIS GUT, HE FOLLOWS THE WORDS OF HIS GUIDE WHO SET HIM ON THIS PATH AND CONTINUES TO STEP FORWARD.

THERE'S A LOT TO DISCOVER ALONG THE WAY.

CHAPTER 4
SUPPORTING ROLES

"WE ARE GROOT."

~Groot, Guardians of the Galaxy

Why are we starting this section with Supporting Roles and not the Hero? As you start your quest into the unknown you will need support, and you need to know that you are never alone regardless of how you feel.

The quest can be long and arduous, stretching you beyond what and who you have been so far. You will have moments you want to cry, moments you want to scream, and moments when you feel your heart could burst from joy. Having the right people around you will give you a safe place to express emotions, to bounce ideas off of, and sometimes to simply be present with.

It's important to know there are many people who play different roles to help you along your quest: the Mentor, Teammates, Sidekicks, Friends, and Fans. Once you become aware of the effect the people around you have, you will know how to be intentional with those relationships.

THE MENTOR

Definition of a mentor: an experienced and trusted advisor, to advise or train (especially a younger colleague).

Mentors are always in a hero story. Joseph Campbell in his "*12 Stages of a Monomyth*" referred to them as Spiritual Aids. Mentors give us their wisdom of how life has worked for them, what they've learned, what they know about the enemy, and how you fit in the big picture. Mentors show up because we are never meant to fight our battles alone.

Mentors show up in the story of superheroes in different forms: wise old sage, an older-generation superhero, an uncle, dad, aunt, oracle, mythological god, sometimes even a child can provide wisdom to guide the hero on his or her path.

Some instances of mentor moments in superhero stories...

Peter Parker had just been bitten by a radioactive spider and was on his way to becoming Spiderman when his uncle, Ben, says, "With great power comes great responsibility." Shortly after that conversation, Ben was killed. Peter held on to that piece of wisdom throughout his life. When his spider senses tingle because of danger nearby, he jumps into action knowing the responsibility he has using his powers for good.

Johnathan and Martha Kent, adoptive parents of baby Clark who fell out of the sky in a spaceship and had to endure a childhood of weirdness: super strength, speed, heat lasers from his eyes, super cold breath, basic indestructibility. They raised Clark to know humanness even though he was an alien to this world. And now, anytime Superman begins to feel detached from the human relationship, he goes home to be surrounded by his mother's love and advice on how to stay grounded when you are capable of literally flying into space.

Princess Diana of Themyscira (Paradise Island) was raised as an only child on an island of immortal women. She had no lack of mentors to talk to, learn from, train with. This molded her into a fearless, intelligent warrior with a soft heart.

When frail Steve Rogers was chosen for a super-secret government project to create a "Super Soldier," newly naturalized German scientist, Abraham Erskine, made Steve understand he wasn't chosen for his body, but his heart. He wasn't just a great soldier, he was a great man with great strength of character. The process he was about to undertake would make Steve even more of what was already within him. "Good becomes greater. Bad becomes, well, worse," Erskine says to Steve. When the procedure was a success and the scientist lay dying from a bullet wound from a German spy crashing the event, Erskine looks to Steve and simply points to his heart before his last breath. When you watch the movie, you see the look on Steve's face change from loss to a determination to catch the bad guy. That look never leaves Captain America's face.

When he was a young boy, Bruce Wayne's parents were brutally murdered in front of him and one man immediately stepped into his life, Alfred Pennyworth. Alfred was the family butler, with his own amazing story that became threaded into Bruce's life. As Bruce grew up and decided to eradicate the evil in Gotham, he went out to find those people, mentors, who could train him to be everything he needed to be to become the world's greatest detective that strikes fear into the heart of every criminal. When he returned to Gotham to create the identity of Batman, Alfred was his guide and support every day covering his playboy billionaire image, and every night backing up the Batman. Only Alfred could tolerate Batman's sulky disposition while giving him advice.

Ororo Munroe, also known as Storm of the X-Men, relied on Charles Xavier as her mentor. He taught her how to control her powers, how to be confident in herself, strong in her uniqueness, and powerful without having god-like arrogance. Without her level of discipline, through her weather control ability that manipulates entire ecosystems, she could split a planet in half through its own natural disasters.

When Dr. Stephen Strange couldn't heal from surgery after a horrible accident, he learned of a spiritual guru that helped a paralyzed man walk again. He set out to find this spiritual mentor, thinking her method of healing included surgery. To his amazement, not only was there no surgery involved, he was led into a mystical quest to wield the Eye of Agamotto and become a Sorcerer Supreme, protecting the world from unearthly dangers.

Mentors can show up in moments that seem random, they can stay with you throughout your life.

I had an opportunity to have dinner with a corporate attorney during an event in New York years ago. She shared her experience of becoming a senior partner under the mentorship of the firm's founder and gave high praise to his role as a mentor. Then she quickly asked me, "Who's your mentor?" I am sad when I say that I did not have one. I have had horrible bosses, a controlling husband, and deceptive therapists, but never a mentor. I replied to the question, "No one."

What I hadn't realized yet was that I did have mentors - through books, TV shows, and movies. I learned well from watching the experience of others. Some of my favorites through the years are characters like McClintock (John Wayne), Leroy Jethro Gibbs, Wonder Woman, the Duke Family, all the Superfriends, Scarlet O'Hara, Daenryus Targaeon, and historical figures, too: Queen Elizabeth I, Abraham Lincoln, Walt Disney, Dolly Parton and a slew of others that have been instrumental in helping me become me.

Think of a time when you received timely advice or wisdom. How has that moment stuck with you? When has it helped you to make a decision?

THE TEAM-UP

Each of us has our uniqueness - powers, abilities, values, personality, tools, and more. There are times we get to team-up with someone else to take down a bad guy or destroy the alien invasion. Some of the most well-known teams are the Avengers, X-Men, Justice League, and even Guardians of the Galaxy. Each team was put together by a leader (Nick Fury, Charles Xavier, and Bruce Wayne respectively), each individually chosen for their unique qualities that, when combined, can save the world.

Each of these teams is individuals who combine their powers to take care of a world-ending scenario. Each plays their part, saving the innocents, using the technology, someone goes high (usually the one that can fly), someone stays low to throw the villain off balance, and another deals the physical blows with full force. Epic battles need multiple heroes, with each hero playing a part. Watch the first Avengers movie when Loki and the Chitauri (evil aliens) invade New York. Multiple heroes on the ground take their turns securing the civilians, Iron Man and Hawkeye in the skies, Hulk takes on the biggest beasts head-first. Each can switch positions but still use their unique ability to get the job done and ultimately stop Loki and reverse the invasion.

Justice League and the X-Men follow suit with their epic battles and various villains. The team-ups are brilliant and exciting to watch as each member engages their inner hero and steps full-on into battle.

Then there's the Suicide Squad. "I want to put together a team of very bad people that can do a lot of good, " says Amanda Waller, head of Cadmus. This motley crew of misfits: Deadshot, Killer Croc, Captain Boomerang, El Diablo, Slipknot, Harley Quinn, Sgt. Flagg, and Katana, was intentionally put together by Waller to complete an impossible mission. Each was chosen for skills that were going to be needed at various points along the way. To Waller, each was useful but expendable. To the team, they were downright weird and irritating to each other. Non-trusting. Yet, they were thrust together to accomplish something they wanted no part of. Until they were faced with a moment of truth - the truth of themselves. We see glimpses of their backstories up until the scene in the bar when they had all given up on the mission and they are commiserating about their miserable lives and their miserable predicament. Then Harley says the most life-coach-profound thing, "Own. That. Shit. It happened. So what? Now what? Own. That. Shit." That was you then, what kind of person do you want to be now?

Team-ups happen in my life all the time. I join forces with other people on Chamber boards, committees, and professional women organizations. I have been a part of ministries in churches, participated in mission trips, and fundraising efforts for non-profits. I even partnered up with a professional dance instructor to perform in a local "Dancing With The Stars" type charity event. Of course, I dressed as Wonder Woman, my partner Damian was Captain America. We had shields, danced the paso doble, and I spun my heart out without falling on stage. I didn't breathe the whole time! But the charity I danced for, Camp Quality Kentuckiana, was blessed with money for the kids at camp, and hundreds of people learned about this great non-profit.

Think about the teams you are on. What gets accomplished as a group versus just one person?

⭐ SIDEKICKS

The sidekick is different than a team-up in one thing - the hero also holds the role of mentor. The classic superhero example of this is Batman and Robin.

Young Dick Grayson lost his parents in a high-flying circus performance accident. Bruce Wayne was in the audience and watched the tragic event unfold. Learning about Dick and feeling the kindred spirit of tragic loss mixed with the need to avenge his parents' death, Bruce takes in the boy as his ward. It didn't take long for Dick to figure out that Bruce was Batman. Then Bruce decided to give him what he wanted - an apprenticeship. Thus, Dick took on his circus name of Robin as his hero moniker and became Batman's "sidekick" through training, practice, and guidance. The bonus for Robin was also gaining Alfred as a second mentor.

The Green Arrow had Speedy, The Flash had Kid Flash, Aquaman had Aqualad, Wonder Woman even had Wonder Girl. Some sidekicks are relatives, some are not.

Many friends of mine have incredible relationships with their kids. They do all sorts of things together: cooking meals, hiking, shopping, working out, traveling, fishing, hunting, starting businesses, caregiving for loved ones, and other activities. For those parents, their kids are their sidekicks - and they wouldn't have it any other way. They share their wisdom and experience with their kids, the kids are supportive of their parents, and both are made stronger for it.

One of the best organizations that foster the mentor-sidekick relationship is Big Brothers Big Sisters. A friend of mine participated as a Big Sister for years and loved it. She would pick up her "sidekick" each week and take off on an adventure for the afternoon. Sometimes it would be visiting the ice cream shop and recounting the school day, other times it would be bowling with laser lights. Each time they would make memories that would last a lifetime for both of them.

I have had the great honor to be a part of a mentoring program for young professionals. Each one became my sidekick for a few months during the program. It wasn't anything that would rate movie blockbuster spectacular; however, the time we would spend chatting over coffee or deep-diving into career development was always an adventure.

BEST BUDS (a.k.a. Brave and the Bold)

The best friend is a different kind of team-up. Where sidekicks get the hero as a mentor, best friends remember the hero BEFORE they were a hero and still support their seemingly crazy desire to run head-first into battle to save the world.

In the latest version of Marvel's Daredevil, Matt Murdock has a best friend, Foggy, that shares the law practice. For the longest time, Foggy didn't know Matt was the Daredevil. Once Foggy found out, Matt and he went through a period of a tense relationship. Foggy even left the practice. Fast forward to the Defenders series, and the time comes for the team-up of Daredevil, Luke Cage, and Jessica Jones to save the Iron Fist and the rest of New York. Foggy is the one that brings Matt his Daredevil suit, knowing he can't stop him from being who he is. He shows his support for his best friend knowing it could be the last time he sees him.

One of my best friends, Dana, came along in a time in my life when I was really struggling to make it through a bad relationship and she was in a similar space. I was nowhere near being the person I am today. It was a dark time and she was supportive and fun for me in the simple things: a night of movies and kitten cuddles, glasses of wine while pouring out our hearts at the dinner table, and a trip to Disney World to just get away from the crazy in our lives. When I took the steps to make changes in my life to follow my dreams, she was with me and she has been with me all the way. And I've done the same for her while she followed her path of adventure.

Who knew you before you tried to accomplish something new in your life? Who has been with you through the adventures?

The FANS

I love my fans! I try to live out the wisdom of Minnie Pearl, "Love your audience and they will love you right back." Fans are a group of people who know you by what you show the world and the value you bring to them. I am a fan of quite a few people: in my industry, in entertainment, and fictional characters like Wonder Woman.

There are pros and cons to having fans.

Pro: there will always be cheers and a wave of the puffy hand to spur you on.

Con: if there is someone or something more

exciting to them, they won't be paying attention to you.

Pro: cheers from fans provide a boost of energy in those moments of weariness.

Con: you can't be sure it's authentic.

Pro: fans will gather to participate in what you are doing or offering.

Con: if you no longer bring them joy and value, they will go somewhere else.

It is good to have fans. Fans give encouragement and validation of a job well done. They rally other fans to your cause. There is a special energy of the combined force of fans. Celebrities use their fan base to launch new music on Twitter. Production studios use superhero fans to develop new movies and merchandise to sell. Businesses have fans that become loyal clients over time.

But remember, fans can be fickle. Unless they have traversed the Quest path and fought alongside you in battle, they don't really know you. In this age of social media madness, fans view your life through soundbites and visual snippets, and those micro-moments are not the real you at the end of a long day.

Fans are worth fighting for, just keep the cheering in perspective.

WHEN IT ALL COMES TOGETHER

Regardless of where we are, the situations we are going through, or what we are trying to accomplish in life, we need other people to be part of our quest.

On a recent CBS Good Morning segment, there was a story of Kathy in Utah. She has multiple sclerosis and 60+ men who put her to bed at night and help her start her day. It started when one neighbor noticed Kathy needed help with a few basic daily functions to improve her quality of life. He began coming in with his wife to help Kathy get ready for bed and then to lift her into the bed to sleep instead of the wheelchair she was in all day. As he would help Kathy, she would share stories of her life before MS.

He quickly realized he was going to need some help to continue assisting Kathy. He gathered a few other men from the neighborhood to help with the lifting. Once the team-up got going and experienced the good they could do for someone else, more wanted to join in. Now, there are over 60 men who spend time with Kathy on a scheduled rotation and help take care of things she needs. There was no money exchanged. This all happened because a man saw a neighbor in need and gathered a team of friends.

Have you heard of the organization B.A.C.A.? Bikers Against Child Abuse. These people come together from all over the world, combining their strengths to team-up for protection and empowerment of children who have been abused. Bikers like John Paul Lilly, put the tough image of a biker to use for good when he founded the organization by coordinating intervention levels that support the abused children. Level 1 is to bring the child into the "family" as an honorary member with a mentor and pictures to remind them they are not alone in their battle. Level 2 has the biker group showing a consistent presence at the home, to be visible at times of vulnerability. Level 3 intervention has the bikers appear in the courtroom - to show solidarity when the child has to publicly stand up to their abuser. B.A.C.A. has developed a creed, and they live by it to answer the Call every time it comes.

As you start your own quest, pay attention to who is around you. They may be a mentor or sidekick, or you may end up being their hero.

CHAPTER 5
WHAT KIND OF HERO ARE YOU?

"YOU CAN TAKE AWAY MY HOUSE, ALL MY TRICKS AND TOYS, BUT ONE THING YOU CAN'T TAKE AWAY - I AM IRON MAN."

~Tony Stark, Iron Man

Throughout history and literature, heroes have come in all types. Some choose to be a hero, some are pushed into the role. The hero types are a reflection of how The Call plays out. There are six basic types, which one(s) do you relate to the most?

The Willing Hero

The Willing Hero has no trouble finding a purpose in life, seeing the vision, doing everything in their power to win the fight, and making sacrifices for the greater good comes naturally to them. Stepping up to protect others and fight the bad guy is what they do. They have no problem leading the team into battle and usually are the ones to provide the inspirational speech.

Steel is a Willing Hero. Superman was killed by the massive mutant enemy called Doomsday and the "Reign of the Supermen" story arc begins with a gap of not having Superman to protect Metropolis. Dr. John Henry Irons remembered a pivotal moment when Superman saved him in the past. When Irons asked how he could repay him, Superman replied, "Live a life worth saving."

Irons, being a genius engineer who is willing to step up to be a hero, builds a mechanized suit of armor that replicates Superman's powers, bears the heroic "S" symbol on his chest, and wields a sledgehammer. Even after Superman comes back (that's a different story arc), Steel helps protect Metropolis and teams up with other heroes to save the day.

The Unwilling Hero

This hero didn't ask to be a hero. Most heroes of this type are passivists and don't want to fight but will do what is necessary when it's called for. Taking the lead, being the first to run into battle, getting excited about the adventure is not really their thing. Even though they don't really want to be considered a hero, doubt and trepidation are their constant companions, they can't walk away from a situation where someone is in trouble. They have a strong inner drive that tells them they need to do the right thing and help. And possibly cuss under their breath while doing it.

In the Marvel universe, Dr. Bruce Banner had the intention of finding out what kind of effect gamma radiation had on people for healing purposes. While testing on himself, things go wrong and he overdoses with gamma rays. He was exposed to enough radiation that when Bruce gets angry he turns into a green monster known as the Hulk. Bruce Banner is a super-intelligent passivist wanting to do good in the world, whereas his alter-ego, the Hulk just likes to smash things. Each time Hulk gets unleashed, Bruce grieves the destruction.

In the DC universe, there is Dove. Dove is the passivist of the duo, Hawk and Dove, who were bestowed powers from mystical beings that mimic chaos and order. Hawk likes to fight and Dove likes to heal.

And as grouchy and egotistical as he can be, Doctor Strange is also a healer and protector more than a run-into-battle type.

The Tragic Hero

This hero type has an origin of tragedy. That tragedy, whether self-induced or circumstance-driven, drives this hero on to make a difference in the world. A sense of redemption fuels this hero.

In his childhood, young Bruce Wayne and his parents were attending a theater show. As they were leaving they were attacked by a robber, both parents were fatally shot, and he was left to hold his dying mother's hand. That moment propelled young Bruce into a definiteness of purpose to fight crime so that no other child would ever have to endure what he went through. There was no end to the adversity Bruce experienced that molded him into the crime-fighting Batman. Years of training, fighting, and continuing to develop his technology and skills made him the greatest detective in the world.

In the CW network version of The Arrow, Oliver Queen was marooned on an island after his father died from their yacht being sabotaged and sank. In his dying words, Oliver's father tells him to fix his mistakes, that he had failed the city, and needed his son to remedy his faults. Oliver comes back to Starling City determined to put right his father's wrongs which included a list of names that needed to be dealt with, and so began Green Arrow's battles.

The Classical Hero

Almost perfect, somewhat innocent, and hard to live up to. These are the characteristics of the Classical Hero type. There is no question these types are comfortable being who they are. There is a strong sense of self and direction in life. They love deeply and live to bring out the best in the world around them.

Seen as being near perfect, always making good decisions, never struggling with much, and the one you always want on your team. When in fact, even though outwardly they may have it all together, this hero's biggest challenge is their inner self - questioning the deeper meanings of life and how they serve others.

Wonder Woman is the Classical Hero. This Princess of Paradise Island was given classic Greek and Roman mythology roots as well as their gifts. Her mother, Hippolyta formed her from clay and the gods gave her the beauty of Aphrodite, the wisdom of Athena, the speed of Mercury, and more strength than Hercules.

In a retelling of her origin, Batman and Superman meets a "new to 'Man's World'" Wonder Woman for the first time. Superman is clearly impressed and Batman dons his normal scowl and growls, "I don't know." Superman presses to get Batman to agree that Wonder Woman is the real deal and someone to include in the superhero circles when Batman replies, "I don't disagree. What I know is we have a lot of catching up to do." Even Batman saw in Wonder Woman the heroic, near-perfect characteristics that everyone wants to aspire to.

The Epic Hero

This hero type laughs in the face of danger, runs toward it, looks forward to standing up to the bully, is always up for a challenge - the more honorable and duty-filled, the better. This hero is physically stronger than most and enjoys a good fight that shows off that strength - the bigger the monster, the better. Songs will be sung about the battles and revelry is planned after every adventure. You might get them confused with the Willing Hero. The difference is the Epic Hero is a little over-the-top.

I think of Thor as the Epic Hero. Thor is part of Norse mythology-turned-superhero. Son of Odin the Norse God and King of Asgard, Thor is a warrior born of royalty and magical lineage. He has incredible strength, can manipulate lightning, and yields the magical hammer, Mjölnir (mewl-near), that serves as a tool to fly through the air and a conduit for lightning that can disarm an enemy with one blow. Thor's role is to protect the nine realms (including Midgard, aka Earth), and as Prince of Asgard, serve as a royal representative.

Everything Thor does is a little more than you would expect. For instance, instead of using the microwave to cook popcorn, he uses a lightning bolt, or smashing the mug and yelling, "Another!" after downing a satisfying cup of coffee. Thor will begin a new fight with a battle cry "For Midgard!" and end it with "Foolish Mortal." He constantly declares the "might of Mjölnir" as if it's his sidekick with a mind of its own and he loves to battle worthy opponents – the bigger the better. Even during the movie, Thor: Ragnorok, Thor banters with the massive demon Surtur while being chained as a prisoner:

> *Thor: "It looks like I'm going to have to choose option b where I bust out of these chains, knock that tiara off your head, and stash it away in Asgard's vault."*
>
> *Surtur: "You cannot stop Ragnorok, why fight it?"*

*Thor: "Because. That's what heroes do."
(enter Mjölnir, the chains break, Thor is free).*

Surtur: "You are making a mistake, Odinson."

Thor: "I make mistakes all the time. Everything seems to work out." (As Thor proceeds to whoop-up on a myriad of large hell-beasts to then take Surtur's "tiara" back to Asgard).

Because that's what Epic Heroes do.

The Antihero Hero

These hero types are the ones that are rough around the edges. Their weaknesses are visible and concentrate more on self-preservation but will step into heroic moments almost begrudgingly.

Deadpool, Wolverine, Rocket (the "raccoon"), and Black Widow. Each of these heroes is not what you would immediately think of when thinking "superhero," but they still qualify as being super.

The type doesn't determine whether or not you have hero material within you. The various types show that a hero can come from any situation and background. Even you.

CHAPTER 6
DISCOVERING WHAT YOU'RE CAPABLE OF

"YOU ARE MUCH STRONGER THAN YOU THINK YOU ARE, TRUST ME."

~Superman

There's a moment in the Wonder Woman movie that sets the tone for this chapter. Diana's aunt, Antiope, has been training her - hard - for years. The Amazons are pushing Princess Diana to her limits as Antiope yells, "Harder! You are stronger than this, Diana". When Diana shifts her gaze for a split second to search for her mother's approval, Antiope attacks, "Never let your guard down. You expect the battle to be fair. The battle will never be fair!" In a move to defend herself, Diana crosses her arms, clashing her warrior bracelets together. The resulting blast was enough to put all the Amazons on their back. Diana, shocked by what just happened, looks at her own hands in absolute surprise coupled with understanding that what just happened came from inside her. From that moment, she continued to test her skills and strengthen her resolve in her mission to reach her destiny in defeating Ares.

There comes a point in our lives when we surprise ourselves with how much we CAN do.

There have been many times in my life when I've had to figure something out. Like a new computer program, or how to change a tire, or how to have a hard conversation that had the potential to ruin lives, or how to get out of debt, or how to start a business, or how to write a book, or many other things that just didn't come naturally to me. Each time I managed to accomplish something and I surprised myself. I didn't know I had it in me to do anything more than answer phones and type memos. Or at least that's what I was led to believe by former bosses and the people around me in the world I grew up in.

In high school, I attended drum major camp. It was a week of standing at attention for hours, waving my arms in tempo for even more hours, and learning about success principles for the first time in my life. Our trainer was the University of Michigan's Director, George Parks. His favorite phrase to get us to pay attention was, "star thought." Each time he said that we would all quickly grab our pencils and notepads to jot down every word we could catch. He gave us the tools we needed to get better at standing in front keeping tempo for a field of musicians and entertainers, work with the band director as an assistant, and be a force for good within the organization (while not abusing our leadership role). One other tool he gave us - the power of individuality.

Being an individual may sound obvious, but not many people are aware they are, and even more, don't know how to be an individual intentionally. That's one of the fun things about superheroes.

There's no getting around their individuality.

Since that first exposure to "star thoughts" in high school I have been on a journey to learn all I can about how people think, believe, and behave so I know better how to help them see their own potential and act on it (and also figure myself out in the process). That journey has been filled with concepts and tools that have helped me design my own uniqueness, and my business that's a beautiful mix of services that fuel strategy for leaders, teams, and businesses.

There is a universal concept I learned through training as an executive coach that rings true every day - WHO we are determines WHAT we do and HOW we do it. If you picture these three as gears working together, the grease that keeps them turning smoothly is the WHY we do it all. It's the central point that allows us to question ourselves, make changes, and define our purpose.

There are a LOT of elements that make us WHO we are:

- Personality
- Gender
- Ethnicity
- Generation
- Geographical location

- Education level
- Income level
- Core values
- Beliefs
- Religion
- Culture
- Family birth order
- Skillset
- Talents
- Enjoyments
- Astrological sign
- Learning style
- Preferences (colors, flavors, music, etc.)
- Messages

Most of these are changeable with intentionality and a plan. All of these details make up your uniqueness. These many factors make you and me complicated human beings. This is also why I strongly believe we are created beings. As the Psalmist says, "knit together in my mother's womb." There's no way I'm an accident and neither are you. I may not have been planned by my parents, but I am certainly no accident. I was created to create, and the more I can discover and understand myself, the more confident I am when a new adventure comes my way.

You can be more confident, too.

Some of these elements seemed obvious when I

first started writing this book. I'm a woman, an only child born in generation "X," lived in a rural location, and I prefer country music, fried chicken, and sweet tea. But wait, things change. Fast forward a handful of years. I now live in the suburbs, and my preferences have added superhero movie soundtracks, interesting salads, and bourbon. We do change, and when we tap into our uniqueness and plan with intention, that change can impact the world in amazing ways by how we live out our adventures.

In our society today we are bombarded with messages that tell us what we "should" be and what we should accept as a new societal norm. You've already thought of at least three examples that have affected you or irritated you. The beauty of understanding the quest portion of the hero's journey is once you've become intentional and aware, you can take control of your life instead of letting life happen to you.

Let's look at some of the main elements that create an intentional awareness of your inner hero's foundation.

 CORE VALUES

Core values are those important, sometimes intangible, things drive us like family, honor, respect, excellence, and a host of other options. Most of the time we don't pay attention to things like values until we feel attacked. Then the core values act as a button that someone keeps pushing over, and over, and over.

Below is a list of values. Which ones are important to you?

Accomplishment	Absence of pain	Abundance
Achievement	Adventure	Altruism
Autonomy	Avoidance of conflict	Beauty
Clarity	Commitment	Communication
Community	Connecting to Others	Creativity
Emotional Health	Environment	Excellence
Family	Flexibility	Freedom
Friendship	Fulfillment	Fun

Holistic Living	Honesty	Humor
Integrity	Intimacy	Joy
Leadership	Loyalty	Nature
Openness	Orderliness	Personal Growth
Partnership	Physical Appearance	Power
Privacy	Professionalism	Recognition
Respect	Romance	Safety
Security	Self-Care	Self-Expression
Self-Mastery	Self-Protection	Self-Realization
Sensuality	Service	Spirituality
Trust	Truth	Vitality

Out of the above, list your Top 5...

These values become the foundational elements that bring you to life.

This is the stuff that means something to you as you go about your day.

Now that you have defined it, you're aware. You'll start to see how these values play out in the world around you.

BELIEFS

Belief is more than what you believe spiritually. What you believe about your values and the world around you affects everything.

The Oxford Dictionary definition of belief is:

A STRONG FEELING THAT SOMETHING/ SOMEBODY EXISTS OR IS TRUE; CONFIDENCE THAT SOMETHING/SOMEBODY IS GOOD OR RIGHT.

You have defined your values. Now what do you believe about them?

After doing these exercises with thousands of people over the years one of the consistent top values is family. Even though multiple people have the same value, what they believe about that value can differ. Some believe that family means everyone gets together every Sunday, have lunch after church, and never have hard conversations that cause conflict. Others believe family is what you give every waking moment to and life revolves around to the detriment of their health and well-being. Others believe that no matter what someone has done (jail, addiction, etc.) if they are family, they are supported regardless of the cost in money or emotional energy. And some believe in healthy boundaries, balanced quality time, and being real with each other. Each looks different even though the values are the same.

Think about finances. Do you believe money is the source of real power in the world? Do you believe it provides security? Do you believe there's not enough? Do you believe that money is just a resource? Do you believe money is the scorecard in the game of life? Some love money. Some hate it. What you believe about it affects how you behave with it.

What about relationships? Pets? Home? Food? Career? Entertainment? Down time? Politics? Younger generations? Older generations? New technology? History?

What you value, drives you. What you believe affects how you behave.

PERSONALITY

One of the most entertaining activities I do with people when guiding them through self-discovery is personality assessments. The comments when it all makes sense to them are varied "No wonder my husband acts like that!" "Huh, maybe I should lighten up when I ask something so she doesn't think I'm trying to attack." "OMG that is so me!" There are some introspective moments and a LOT of laughter.

Personality assessments and studies have been around for decades. There are many different ones to choose from and all center around helping people understand the differences in how we present ourselves in the world.

How you live out your core values and beliefs plays out through your personality.

There are four base personality types. Similar to the basic food groups, personalities can include a slew of sub-sections. Mashing together elements from each group can make a well-balanced dish. What does your personality plate look like?

GROUP 1

This group has high dominant traits. That's why in the DISC assessment this group is known as dominant. But others may label them Type A, a Lion, Ruby, Powerful, etc. Traits include:

- Take-charge kind of person - when everyone else takes too long to make a move, they're on it.
- Typically the leader of the pack and have no qualms with taking risks.
- Their communication style is direct.
- Their strength out of balance includes insensitivity.

GROUP 2

These are the people who love fun and hate being tethered. Being high influencers for their excitement, like a great entertainer, their labels include Influencer, Otter, Sapphire, Popular, etc. Traits include:

- Social butterfly - never met a stranger and can talk to a post.
- They will dream bigger than anyone

else - very creative.
- Their communication style is high energy and enthusiastic.
- Their strength out of balance includes lack of follow-through.

GROUP 3

The Golden Retrievers. This group has high-level loyalty. They are the steady ones, which is why in DISC their label is Steadiness, other labels include the Pearls and Peaceful. Traits include:

- They nurture - first motivation is to keep everyone peaceful and pleased.
- They enjoy routine and security.
- Their communication style is two-way, great listeners.
- Their strength out of balance includes the inability to say "NO."

GROUP 4

This group loves detail, the more the better. You

find them as accountants, architects, and researchers. Labels for them include Conscientiousness, Beaver, Emeralds, Perfectionists, etc. Traits include:

- Industrious and analytical - they love to work out the flowcharts or numbers.
- They are great at quality control.
- Their communication style is factual and precise.
- Their strength out of balance includes negativity.

When I teach about personality traits, I point out that everyone has elements of each group inside them. The dominant personality type is what shows up in high-stress moments - both happy and not so happy moments. On a normal day and in mundane moments, we fluctuate between two majors and minors, or all four evenly.

What does it look like when a beaver and lion are fused? An analytical "Type A" that may communicate a lot of detail with bluntness and process. What about the otter and golden retriever? A spontaneous high-energy people-pleaser. Lion and golden retriever? A "Type A" that puts others before themselves and can get their feelings hurt easily. There are a lot of combinations, each one unique.

What you value, drives you. What you believe affects how you behave. Your personality is how you express it all.

SKILLS & TALENTS

Talent is a natural skill.

Skill is the ability to do something well, or at a level of expertise.

There are people out there who have tons of talent in an area we only dream of being good in. We look at them with awe and wonder, and sometimes a little envy. Then there are those we seem to barely notice until there's a crisis. That's when their special skillsets kick in to save all of us by keeping the supply chain running smoothly during global pandemics.

Everyone has a talent for something, and everyone is needed for what their talents bring to the world around them.

Skills can be taught and developed over time. So

even if you have a natural skill for something (talent), you can still develop that skill over time to master an area of your life.

In the superhero world talents can look, well, super:

FLIGHT
STRENGTH
INVISIBILITY
MIND CONTROL
TELEKINESIS
WEATHER CONTROL
TELEPORTATION
INVULNERABILITY
SONIC SCREAMS

In our everyday world, talents are a different version of super:

Singing
Painting
Mechanics
Gardening
Cooking
Dancing
Golfing
Reading people
Working with animals
And so on...

Wonder Woman is a natural leader - that's talent. She is a warfare master that was trained from childhood to develop skills necessary to fight for peace.

Tony Stark is a tech genius - that's talent. Iron man is not very skilled at playing well with others. He needed help from the other Avengers which helped him develop into a great father and husband.

Batman is a natural detective - that's talent. His skills were developed as a fighter to instill fear into his enemies.

Storm's natural talent is to control the weather. Her skills of self-discipline keep her from destroying the planet.

There are thousands of people who enjoy running and have the talent to not trip over themselves and others. Yet it takes training to complete a triathlon.

Some enjoy public speaking even if no one is listening. Others need six weeks of preparation to do a one-minute speech.

What talents do you have? It's going to be that

thing that you just do - typically enjoy - without any real effort or thought being put into it.

What skills are you currently developing to reach your goals?

AWARENESS & INTENTION

The thing about discovering what you are capable of, how you are formed as an individual, you are officially aware. What will you do with this newfound awareness?

Develop your inner superhero to take on the villain...

CHAPTER 7
THE VILLAIN

"YOU EITHER DIE A HERO OR LIVE LONG ENOUGH TO SEE YOURSELF BECOME THE VILLAIN"

~Harvey Dent, Two-Face

The air is filled with minor chords. The film filter shifts from warm bright colors to dark and eerie. The room is darker and the feeling is cold, empty, and ominous.

Every quest includes a villain to defeat.

In literature, there is the antagonist, someone who is in opposition to the hero. An antagonist is not always a villain. Villains are not only in opposition to the hero, they also have evil intent.

Villains are hell-bent on causing chaos and destruction. They want ultimate control. They have an intricate plan to take over – long before you know what's happening. They always seem to be two steps ahead of you. There is a confident air of evil surrounding them. They rule others through fear and lack remorse for wrong-doings. They even seem to enjoy making others miserable. Villains are ruthless. Villains are real.

Just like various hero types, there are multiple versions of villains:

- *THE ANTI-VILLAIN:* they don't appear evil, but have evil intentions.
- *THE AUTHORITY FIGURE:* they like to remove free will.
- *THE BEAST:* usually an animal or something from nature (like Jaws shark).

- *THE BULLY:* they're just mean.
- *THE CORRUPTED:* once good, but something happened to make them change.
- *THE CRIMINAL:* they are in it for money and power and will do whatever it takes to get both.
- *THE DISTURBED:* these villains showcase clear inner personality issues.
- *THE EQUAL:* these are those who are pretty much equal to the hero but different morals, values, and ethics.
- *THE FEMME FATALE:* female, seductress, kill-you-in-your-sleep type.
- *THE HENCHMAN:* does the dirty work of the Mastermind.
- *THE MACHINE:* out to destroy humanity because humanity is flawed.
- *THE MASTERMIND:* the brilliant, ruthless character making and organizing the diabolical plans.
- *MOTHER NATURE:* don't piss her off...tornados, tidal waves, earthquakes, you name it.
- *THE PERSONIFICATION OF EVIL:* little to no backstory and every evil deed is motivated by wanting to do evil things.

That's a lot of villain types! Considering there are fewer hero types than villains, it seems a little outnumbered. No wonder we are tired at the end of the day. There's opposition everywhere you turn. As we advance on the quest, there is usually one prominent villain that has to be taken down.

The Joker is Batman's number one nemesis, a maniacal sociopath, that when he is not in the mental asylum for the criminally insane, he is conjuring up schemes to destroy Gotham with his twisted sense of comedy like using poisonous laughing gas. And he always does it with an extra objective to also take out the Batman.

Then there's Lex Luthor. Lex believes he is saving the world through his schemes to destroy Superman, the alien from another world that could turn on us at any moment.

Loki, Thor's adopted brother, is a trickster by nature so scheming to take over Asgard is always part of his day. His scheming to manipulate everyone to do his bidding brings destruction and mayhem everywhere he goes.

Ares, the god of war, seems pretty obvious. He lives for divisiveness and does all he can to thwart Wonder Woman's mission of peace.

Captain America has the Red Skull. Professor X has Magneto. Black Panther has Kilmonger.

There's always one main villain for each quest.

And, sometimes the villains team up and you are faced with fighting more than one at a time.

In my circle of friends and family, some life circumstances are obvious villains:

- Bankruptcy
- Natural disaster
- Suicide or sudden death of a loved one
- Job loss
- Divorce
- Auto accident
- Global pandemics
- and more

For too many in my circle, cancer is the villain. Some have beaten it (sometimes more than once), others have not. For each person, that moment the word comes out of the doctor's mouth their life changes. They get thrown into a quest they didn't ask for and immediately they know what they are fighting. In the process of fighting, they know who their supporters are - the mentors, the sidekicks, the team-ups. They discover more about themselves and how they see the world. They start to engage their inner hero.

Other obvious villains are the difficult people we must engage with at work, in groups, and sometimes at home. Some villains are the people we trusted most that turn on us.

In my history, the men I've been drawn to have had real charisma, high energy, vision-driven goals, and were great to be around. At first. Once we began spending more time together, I learned quickly that they were not what they seemed. Too many times I've gotten myself into relationships thinking it would go great when it turned out they wanted to control me. They worked to separate me from everyone else that could support me - friends, family. They would phrase the words and conversation in a way that made me doubt who I was. There would be times that I would question my own words after a conversation. And everything was always my fault.

Identifying the villain can be tricky.

One of Wonder Woman's worst enemies is Dr. Psycho. And yes, it is as obvious as it sounds. He's a psychopathic psychotherapist that can control people's minds. He has the ability to make this near-indestructible Amazonian Princess experience a different reality through mind manipulation. He has made her life miserable more than once by playing mind games. Making her believe she was timid, weak, and dowdy.

The worst enemy is the one that can create confusion, that can make us doubt ourselves and what we believe in. The one that puts false ideas and messages in our head. Most of the time we think the villain is the circumstance, or a person causing the circumstance, when in fact, the villain is our thoughts. The limiting beliefs we hold, the negative feelings we carry, the abusive conversations we have with ourselves. We are our own worst enemy.

Even now I am still working on the kind of conversations I have with myself. I don't have a lot of nice things to say. I have royally screwed up my life by making all sorts of stupid decisions. You may not think so, but I do. I still relive old hurts and past chaotic situations that wear me out. I woke up one morning noticing that even when I am thankful for all the things I have, like a roof over my head and food in the fridge and great clients to work with and amazing friends, I still gravitate to "that moment" that gets me worked up and pissed off. It could be the way someone treated me in the past or even something that hasn't happened and I've over-analyzed to the point of getting myself into fight mode. It may generate enough energy to get me to the coffee maker in the morning, but it is not the kind of energy I want to carry around. It's not what I want my life to look like.

Thinking so much about all the negative is what holds me back from moving forward to good things in my life.

There's a passage in the Bible (2 Corinthians 10:5) where the Apostle Paul writes to the Christians in Corinth and uses the term, "take every thought captive." That's what you have to do to the villain in your head. Take it captive. Interrogate the crap out of it, and defeat it.

And if it escapes, to attack again, be prepared to go into battle.

 # THE BATTLE

THE TIME HAS COME. THE HERO IS FACE-TO-FACE WITH THE GIANT. THIS IS THE CULMINATION OF THOSE DECISION MOMENTS ALONG THE QUEST. WHAT WILL HAPPEN?

Invariably, the hero takes a beating. This is the defining moment. Has he developed his super self to conquer the giant?

The moment seems bleak. His very soul takes a beating

Until he remembers everything he's fought for along the way. What the importance of the mission is. The impact this moment will have on his world.

He takes a deep breath, screams his battle cry, and advances toward the giant.

Chapter 8
The First Time Out

"I THINK PAIN IS WHAT MAKES YOU A HERO. IT'S LIKE A PRESSURE THAT EITHER FORMS A DIAMOND OR GRINDS YOU INTO DUST. "

~Beast Boy

The battle begins. Enemy forces surround you and there seems to be no way out. You throw a punch, only to have it land like an egg on a brick wall. That hurts enough to make you cry. You try all the moves and tricks and tactics you've learned and nothing helps you win the day. You fight as hard as you can for as long as you can. You're alive, but barely. The enemy has won this battle and you walk away defeated.

Just because you have developed your hero skills does not mean you always win the battle the first time out.

My first attempt to make my dreams come true was when I went off to college. The experience didn't go well and I failed miserably.

I auditioned for vocal performance at Indiana University Bloomington and for a spot in the Color Guard. I was accepted for both! But, because I had never had a formal lesson in my life and had no training about how to deal with emotional adversity, my first experience with a music teacher was horrendous. After the first lesson she told me directly, "You were never meant to be here. You're only here to fill a quota. You are nowhere near talented enough to even be in a chorus group."

I was crushed. I was double-majoring in audio technology and vocal performance, and jumped right into a situation where I didn't know anything about - anything. I didn't even know how to use public transportation to get around the huge campus or to the football fields to practice in Color Guard for the Marching Hundred. I was having anxiety attacks to the point I even lost my hearing for a time. It was all too much. I gave up. I didn't know how to mentally and emotionally go back into battle to fight for my dream.

I came back home, got a job, and did what was expected of me. At that point, my comfort zone was something I didn't know how to grow out of. I knew I wanted to do more with my life than work at a job I didn't like, but what?

When we talk of battles the image that comes to mind is someone fighting in the military. Rarely do they lose a battle the first time out. Why is that? Because they've trained for it, on purpose, for a long time. But even for a military person, not all will win the very first battle of bootcamp.

I have had almost every military friend tell me that bootcamp was the hardest thing they had to do. For them, it's the season of the quest: they find out what they're made of, they develop the team, they follow their leaders, they learn strategy, and they know what or who they are fighting and what the mission will be when they enter battle mode. Those initial months of going through the quest prepare them for the obvious battles out in the world.

But, some enter bootcamp as a battle. They are not open to learning and developing into someone new, stronger, and defined. They struggle the most during bootcamp, and don't make the cut. It's not just about being physically strong to be a hero - it's being mentally disciplined and character-fortified. Those qualities are developed on purpose through training and over time.

In the movie, Avengers - Age of Ultron, the heroes had already worked together to save New York from the alien invasion. They've proven they are heroes. They should win every time, right?

Yes, until they encounter a new foe. Enter Scarlet Witch. Wanda Maximoff, aka Scarlet Witch, has the power to manipulate minds and matter. The Avengers go to Ship Graveyard to find Ultron and put him down, not knowing that Wanda would be there to mess with their heads. Each hero she put into a trance that had them thinking of a skewed past, completely disarming them and causing incredible amounts of chaos while the bad guys escape.

Remember, the worst enemy is the one that causes confusion. And, the mind mash method is timeless. The Superfriends cartoon from the late 1960s had a villain that used a special ray that read the Wonder Twins minds and bring to life their worst fears (some Exxorian monster). There has been Loki, Dr. Psycho, The Scarecrow, and others across the superhero universes. All the way to recent years when Maxwell Lord was using mind control on Superman (imagine what kind of hell that could cause the world - don't worry, Wonder Woman shut that down).

I cannot emphasize enough - *the biggest battles are the battles in our minds.*

When we lose to a circumstance early in our lives (like losing a job or getting rejected by a love interest or friend or family member), it wreaks havoc on our confidence and how we think of ourselves and the world around us. It could cause us to give up and go back to our comfort zone.

On my bio-Dad's deathbed I tried to find out why he never tried to be a father to me. He told me that my mom made it too hard so he gave up. When I asked the harder question about his faith and whether he and I would have a second chance in heaven, he couldn't answer me. He only told me a story of when he was young boy and seeing all the "church folk" in the bars with his own dad, who was belligerent and abusive. That's when he gave up on church and God. Giving up was his pattern. John Smallwood died at the age of 54 from alcoholism, never knowing how to live or love.

You've been called to something great: parenting, business ownership, community involvement, fostering, cause-fighting and so on. Answer the Call, go on the quest, and stay focused on why you're doing it. If we lose focus - we lose the battle. My bio-dad never really had a focus. He never answered the Call to something greater than himself and more people than just himself suffered for it.

There will always be challenges during the battle. The rescue helicopter that gets struck by lightning. The cord isn't long enough to connect two world-saving satellites. The needed technology to save the day suddenly breaks down. The vial of a fast-spreading virus accidently breaks in the lab. A team member has their own challenges that cause them to be late to help you. Challenges are part of the battle. Staying super-focused allows energy and space to go back at it to win the next time.

In my world of business ownership and leadership, I have studied the Super people who have gone before me for decades now. Here are some great examples of hitting a brick wall early on in their journeys:

Walt Disney was told by his editor boss that he lacked imagination and had no creativity.

Colonel Sanders failed at multiple businesses. He travelled from one side of the country to the other to find someone to buy his Kentucky Fried Chicken to serve in their restaurant. He was in his 60s.

Sir James Dyson had 5,216 failed attempts and 15 years at developing what would become the best-selling bagless vacuum cleaner.

Rejected twice by the University of Southern California's School of Cinematic Arts, Steve Spielberg went on to gross more money than you can probably count from all the successful blockbuster movies.

Thomas Edison was told by his teachers that he was "too stupid to learn anything." Bet they didn't get a discount for that first practical electric lamp or phonograph!

As a child, Albert Einstein didn't start speaking until he was FOUR! They thought he was mentally handicapped. He might have been thinking of the right first word.

You know that author, the one who wrote Harry Potter? J.K. Rowling was broke, divorced, depressed, and a single mom before going on to become one of the richest women in the world.

Jerry Seinfeld's first time on stage he froze and the audience booed him off the stage.

Oprah was fired from her first job as a TV anchor in Baltimore.

"You should go back to driving a truck," was what Elvis Presley was told after his first appearance on the Grand Ole Opry.

There are COUNTLESS examples of early battles lost by highly successful people. They didn't lose focus. They didn't give up. One of the most used quotes about adversity is from Michael Jordan,

"I have missed more than 9,000 shots in my career. I have lost almost 300 games. On 26 occasions I have been entrusted to take the game winning shot, and I missed. I have failed over and over and over again in my life. And that is why I succeed."

95

Battle is part of the journey of Being Super. The important thing to know is that when you are faced with a set-back you don't let it keep you back there. You have a reason to keep going.

Chapter 9
Purpose Found

"LIFE DOESN'T GIVE US PURPOSE. WE GIVE LIFE PURPOSE."
                                    ~Barry Allen, The Flash

After their yacht was shipwrecked, Robert Queen's last words to his son was, "Survive. Right my wrongs." From there, former playboy Oliver Queen was thrown into a five-year quest to get back home to bring retribution to those on his father's list of wrong-doers as the Green Arrow.

Purpose in life doesn't always come quickly nor is it always obvious. Even Mother Teresa didn't know her real purpose until she answered the call to become a nun.

Knowing at age 12 she wanted to become a missionary, Agnes Gonxha Bojaxhiu in Skopje, Macedonia, joined the Sisters of Loreto in Ireland. After her time as a novitiate, she was sent to serve in a missionary convent in Calcutta, India. Seeing the suffering and poverty all around her, she was moved to make a difference. That Call within a Call became her life's purpose to love and care for those who no one else was prepared to serve. Her purpose caused a ripple effect when she created The Missionaries of Charity that grew to an International organization with millions of people working across the world.

Now mind you, not all of us are Nobel Prize-Winning Saints. But we all have a purpose that can create a ripple effect. And often that purpose is found in the battle time.

Myles was a truck driver when I first met him at our coaching class. He had driven big rigs for most of his life and was taking the training to become something new for his retirement years. Going through training to become a certified coach is not easy. The internal battles that are fought test your will to keep going. Myles never gave up. His initial plan was to coach truck drivers that wanted to be more focused on setting and hitting goals because that was the world he knew. What he found was that there were many people like him who wanted to do something different in life. He found his purpose in being a transition coach that helps people go from one career to another and to find their purpose in life.

Going through the adversity of battle makes you stronger. No, it doesn't feel like it, but it does make you stronger.

"I shouldn't be alive, unless it was for a reason. I know what I have to do, and I know it is right," Tony Stark shared with his friend. Tony became Iron man after his Army escort was blown up by his own company's weapons. Then he was taken by terrorists to develop a weapon for them. Instead of developing a new terrorist weapon he created a suit of armor to use to escape. From there, Tony went on to change the direction of his worldwide company from weapons manufacturing to energy innovation.

Out of trial and tribulation, purpose can be found.

From all my studies I have discovered three main themes of purpose:

REDEMPTION - TO RIGHT A WRONG
MAKING THE WORLD SAFE
MAKING THE WORLD BETTER

Darnell Ferguson, owner of SuperChef, encompasses all three.

Darnell always had a love for creating great meals and worked his way through school to graduate from the Sullivan University in Kentucky with a Degree in Culinary Arts. But because of some bad decisions and life situations he found himself homeless, in and out of jail, and unemployed.

Not wanting to be another statistic with a criminal record, he put his faith in God and his creative cooking abilities into action to bring a high-end breakfast pop-up restaurant concept to life. He saw a lot of growth quickly and was able to open his own restaurant, SuperChefs. The momentum didn't stop there and neither did the adversity. A few short months after he opened his first restaurant, it burned down. A complete loss. The news hit the airwaves and got the attention of celebrity chefs and television producers to encourage Darnell to share his story.

From that outpouring of support, Darnell was able to rebuild and even expand. While rebuilding, he got involved with non-profit groups like Blessings in a Backpack and Children Shouldn't Hunger, serving on their board and providing meals to children.

"The difference between where I was at and where God wanted me to be was based on my ability to patiently suffer. I went through it knowing I could come out the other side."

Darnell found purpose through his pain by utilizing his experience and gifts to feed others with inspiration and creative food in Super environments. He found redemption in building a new life through a career he loves. He makes the world safe through making sure kids are fed. He makes the world better through his innovative approach to the food experience and inspiration of his own turn-around.

From <*http://www.iamsuperchef.com/about-us/*>

Every superhero has a purpose to make what went wrong turn right, to protect those who can't protect themselves, and to make the world better. But when going through the battle, it isn't always easy to see the purpose. That's when you need to get your team to help you regroup.

Chapter 10
Regroup

"SOLDIERS TRUST EACH OTHER.
THAT'S WHAT MAKES US AN ARMY."
                ~Steve Rogers, Captain America

There's a scene in the first Guardians of the Galaxy movie where the group of ex-con misfits have just had their asses handed to them in battle.   They all feel defeated and miserable. Then Peter Quill stands and says,

"I look around at us and you know what I see? Losers. I mean, like, folks who have lost stuff. And man, we have all of us. Our homes, our families. Normal lives.   And usually life takes more than it gives, but not today. Today it has given us something. It has given us a chance."

Drax looks at Quill like he's just lost his mind and responds, "To do what?"

Quill, "To give a shit, for once, and not run away.   But I, for one, am not going to stand by and watch Ronin kill billions of people."

Rocket chimes in, "But Quill, you're asking us to die."

"Yeah, I guess I am."

There's a moment of internal consideration when Gamora breaks the silence, "Quill, I have lived most of my life surrounded by my enemies, I will be grateful to die among my friends."

Drax joins in, "You're an honorable man, Quill. I will fight beside you. In the end, I will see my wife and daughter again."

Of course, Groot says, "I am Groot."

Everyone looks at Rocket to get his response, "Oh what the hell, I don't have that long of a life span anyway."

There's a period of regrouping after battles that allows you to breathe for a moment and regain energy from your support team. They help you see things you may have missed about the villain. They help you refocus on the areas in which you excel. They ask the hard questions that help you get answers. They remind you what you are capable of and your purpose.

What were you programmed to do?

Part of regrouping from a battle is reviewing what you did in the situation. Followed by the classic question ask yourself, "What in the world was I thinking?" We've discussed in previous chapters how important your thoughts are. It matters even more in the midst of battle.

Review your thought habits. Spend time thinking about what you've been thinking about. Does it help you handle adversity, or does your thoughts make situations worse?

You may have grown up adopting other people's way of thinking. Are those thought patterns helpful or hurtful?

You may have never paid attention to what you think. It's possible that you only act on emotion. Has that method worked for you when dealing with challenges?

Who do you THINK you are?

Every superhero has an identity crisis. This time of regrouping gives you the space to be reminded by your team who you are and how you show up in the world.

They remind you so you can remind yourself.

Questioning 'who am I' is natural. It's when you start doubting yourself your internal villain appears. Doubt is a very real enemy.

So, stop doubting yourself. Now.

If you are struggling with those thoughts that are downers, remember to "take every thought captive" and interrogate the crap out of it. Find out why that thought has appeared and what mission it is trying to accomplish. If the mission is to destroy you – time to destroy it.

As you regroup and ask yourself deep questions, you have the ability to accept thoughts that make you better and reject those that tear you down.

How are you managing the emotions?

Every time a battle arises, so do the emotions. Emotions fuel your powers. Without direction, emotions take over and get in the way at the moments you need to keep controlled. So, what do you do? Find your way to managing the emotions.

In the movie, X-Men First Class, a young Charles Xavier is training Erik Lensherr (Magneto) to use his power of metal manipulation from long distance. Xavier tells him that true focus lies somewhere between rage and serenity, and after accessing Erik's memories to show him, he goes on to say, "There's so much more to you than you know, not just pain and anger. There is good, too. When you can access all of that, you can access a power no one can match. Not even me."

In the animated series, Avengers Assemble, each Avenger has their own space in Avengers Tower. Hulk's space is filled with miniature glass figures and a water fountain. It's the space where he balances his emotions and finds peace while knowing if he is out of balance, the glass figures he holds dear will shatter.

Raven is a character with the Teen Titans whose father is the demon Trigon who tried to use his own daughter as a portal to the human world to destroy it. Daddy issues don't even begin to cover it. Raven's non-fight time is spent largely in meditation to control her thoughts and emotions so she doesn't turn into her father.

Find your space, go there, get control.

Do you have a plan?

My friend, Charlene, is a fabulous pool player: tournament winner, trophies on the wall, brought home money kind of pool player. One thing she's taught me about playing pool is that it involves strategy. You are not making that shot just to get the ball in a pocket. You are making that shot to set up for the next shot. Sometimes, you don't want to make the object ball, but instead want to prevent your opponent from making their object ball.

There's always a strategy to winning the game, whatever game that is: basketball, chess, business, surgery, life.

Your support system is there to help you with a strategy that empowers you to plan the best moves to win the battle.

Do you even have to fight?

There is an episode of the Justice League Unlimited animated series here Hawk and Dove team up with Wonder Woman to fight an indestructible suit of armor that moves on its own and is imbued with power from the war god, Ares. Wonder Woman figured out the armor was fueled by rage (something Ares loves). As the armor approaches a group of soldiers, Dove moves between the two and simply stands in front of the moving armor. Hawk screams for his brother to move while Wonder Woman restrains him. As the scene unfolds, the armor no longer fueled with the hate energy, shuts down.

"Sometimes it takes more strength NOT to fight." Wonder Woman says. And it all makes sense.

There will be battles that we cause on our own through those heightened negative emotions. Finding the peace to not rage will help create stability in the situation, and may very well stop the battle altogether.

The regrouping time is important for what's to come.

Chapter 11
When All Hope Seems Lost

"THERE ARE DAYS THAT TEAR HOPE DOWN AND STOMP ON IT...BUT EVEN ON THOSE DAYS, WE CAN STAND UP. WE CAN FIGHT. WE CAN RISE."

~Sam Wilson, The Falcon

The music swells. Senses are heightened. No team. No mentor. No Sidekick. There is destruction all around. Victory seems impossible. All hope seems gone. All that's left is you and the enemy in front of you.

What do you do?

There was a point in my life where I had lost everything within a four-month time span. I was living with my best friends. They decided to divorce and go their separate ways. Neither claimed me in their divorce - a 20-year friendship (and their even longer marriage) gone with a swish of a pen. My business partner turned on me. He went from being an equal partner to treating me as a subordinate and then undermining my efforts with our clients – followed by walking out on the business and leaving me with a financial mess. My business was in shambles. My truck died. I lost my home. I had to find a new family for my cats. I filed bankruptcy. My health gave out. My bank account was empty. I felt alone. I felt like a massive failure. I had no energy, no smile, no vision, no hope.

It sucked. Beyond sucked. I was living out a bad country song. And no one really knew the magnitude of what was happening at the time. To me it felt like a hopeless situation.

There comes a point in every hero story, your story, when all hope seems lost. Everything that could go wrong does. Over and over and over again. It's the point where it's difficult for you to take a breath, let alone think clearly enough to figure out what to do. You can barely move. Barely speak. Every fiber of your being is ready to shatter.

And there it is...the defining moment.

DEFINING MOMENTS & BATTLE CRIES

The defining moment is the turning point. Everything changes from that moment. It's based on one person's decision - yours.

Will you get up and fight with all you have?

Or will you run away, destined to relive the same battle again and again?

Superheroes wouldn't be super if all they did was run when hope seemed lost. They muster their last ounce of courage to generate action through fear. And every time, the hero steps a little further into their potential. Sometimes in slow-motion.

Think about it. The defining moment is so defining that the movie director has made it a slow-motion moment. The hero's theme music starts to play the distinct tones. The lighting changes. The whole theater knows the game just changed from all hope lost to the villain's going down!

The defining moment can be freeing.

"THERE'S A MOMENT WHEN SHE'S OUTRUN EVERY DOUBT AND FEAR SHE'S EVER HAD ABOUT HERSELF, AND SHE FLIES. IN THAT MOMENT EVERY LITTLE GIRL FLIES."
-CAROL DANVERS, 2015 CAPTAIN MARVEL

Carol Danvers went through a lot of adversity to become Captain Marvel. And after, while stranded on Earth fighting a shape-shifting alien race known as the Skrull, she discovered what she had been told on the Kree military force was all a lie. After being captured by those she thought she could trust, she learned she had more power than she ever imagined. Her defining moment came when she faced her mind-controlling captor and told herself, "I've been fighting with one hand tied behind my back. I wonder what would happen if I was finally set free." Carol tapped into that inner power to explode her chains and ultimately defeat the entire Kree military invasion.

A defining moment is never about logical systems and approaches - it's pure emotional energy.

You feel it in your gut.

You refuse to be defeated. You refuse to stay down.

You begin to act on instinct. You know what to do. You've already discovered your talents, honed your skills, and know the mission.

You run. Not away from the fight. You run toward it.

Like my friend Virginia would say before entering a battle, "hold my earrings."

I had to learn that the hard way with relationships.

Over and over I would run away from dealing with toxic people. Whether it was my dad, boyfriend, husband, boss, business partner, it didn't matter. They were all horrible relationships. And that's a nice way to put it. For each of those relationships I thought for years the problems were all my fault. That I was the horrible person. That I was everything they said I was, "a stubborn bitch," "ridiculous," "will never be successful," "useless," "waste of space," "stupid," "too emotional," and other things that give you an idea that it wasn't healthy conversations. The thing is - I just took what they said. I took it all to be true and did everything within my power to NOT be those things. Not because I was motivated to be better, to live out my potential. But because I wanted to outrun my shame of even being born.

And when I couldn't outrun my shame, I was susceptible to any man telling me something good about myself while secretly having bad intentions. Then I would be right back down that same battle path. I finally got to a point where I felt hopeless about relationships. I saw no use for them and the idea of being in one made me miserable. And when I found out the last man I was with was only trying to make another woman jealous, it was more than I could take.

It became a defining moment. Was I going to run away or deal with it?

I stopped. I was done rationalizing his actions as rational. I was done believing the lies. I was done feeling like I was the one in the wrong. I was done feeling like I was worthless. I stopped. I addressed how his behavior made me feel. He brushed it off as a bad mood. When his number showed up on my phone again, I didn't answer it. It wasn't long before the phone stopped ringing.

I walked away and haven't looked back. I've taken the time to rediscover myself. To focus my energy into my business, this book, my support system.

My life is filled with failures that made me feel like all hope was lost:

- I failed miserably in my childhood with family members that didn't want me around.
- I failed miserably when I left home to go to a college I wasn't prepared to experience.
- I failed miserably when I married the man who convinced me It was my last chance (at age 23) to "have it all."
- I failed miserably when I took the abuse.

- I failed miserably when I kept going back to those same type of men after my divorce.
- I failed miserably when I chose to work entry-level jobs and think that was all I was qualified for.
- I failed miserably when I allowed yet another man convince me that he would make us successful in business and then convinced me it was all my fault it failed.
- I failed miserably when my friend of 20 years texted me to move out before her divorce, "I've helped you all I can."
- I failed a lot.

But with each of those failures, those "all hope seems lost" moments, there was always a point when I surrendered to my faith. In those moments I believed I had nowhere else to go except to cry out to God to save me. Sometimes in dramatic moments face-down on the bathroom floor because it was the only door that could be locked and private in the house.

My internal battle cry became, "HELP!" Followed by "ENOUGH!"

And in a split second, peace. Peace enough to take a next breath, a next step.

Being on this side of all the adversity, I know for

certain it was in those defining moments when I leveled up to become something more.

A sacrifice made for the greater good

You might think defining moments have to be major events. Sometimes they are the kind that requires huge sacrifice.

Thor knew when he walked down Main Street to face the giant soulless machine, he would need to sacrifice his life for all the others. Through the quest of getting his hammer and to go home to Asgard - the battle of disappointment in knowing he can't - brought him to a new level of quiet confidence in the purpose of being the leader that serves and sacrifices, not just rushes in without thought. In that defining moment of battle with The Destroyer, Thor takes his last breath proving he is worthy of the power of Thor and his hammer, Mjolnir, returns to him bringing life force with it.

The ensuing scenes show his full god-like strength and power destroying the machine as only Thor could and continuing on to an epic battle with his brother, Loki, where he makes the choice to sacrifice his love on Earth for the safety of the people of Asgard and the 9 realms.

In the movie "Superman v. Batman, Dawn of Justice," after Wonder Woman and Batman fight their hardest against the Doomsday creature, only Superman could destroy it. In the process of destroying the monster, Superman died and the world mourned. But that emblem on his chest wasn't an "S." It was Kryptonian for "Hope." That emblem inspired others to take up the mantle of a hero to continue in Superman's footsteps.

Every actor that plays a hero is affected by the role. Christopher Reeve was no exception. He played the role of Superman through the 70s and 80s in multiple movies. The distinguishing musical tones of up, up, and away run through the theme music. And the scene where he meets Lois Lane for the first time - as Clark Kent, then as Superman - was romantic and incredible. For a whole generation of people, Christopher Reeve WAS Superman.

And that's why so many were stunned the day Superman stopped flying.

In 1995 Reeve experienced a horse riding accident. He suffered a spinal cord injury and was rendered paralyzed from the neck down. Superman may have stopped flying, but it didn't stop him from being a superhero.

Reeve and his wife, Dana, went on to create the Christopher & Dana Reeve Foundation in 1998 to promote research into spinal cord injuries. He also appeared and testified before a Senate subcommittee in favor of federal funding for stem cell research. Even after his death in 2004, his passion for innovation toward a cure and a vision to provide resources for those paralyzed along with their caregivers, continues to give hope to the paralysis community all over the world.

In the Wonder Woman movie there is a moment when Diana, in the heat of battle with Ares, is holding a tank above her head ready to crash it down on Doctor Poison's head while Ares is yelling for her to kill the Doctor. In that moment, looking into the Doctor's eyes, she has flashbacks that lead her through her conversation with Steve Trevor where Steve tells her, "I can save today. You can save the world...I love you." She reminds herself (while still holding the tank) of all that she's learned and experienced in "Man's World." She takes a breath, puts down the tank, then proceeds to thoroughly defeat Ares - the true villain of the story - while telling him, "It's not about what you deserve. It's about what you believe. I believe in love."

Not every defining moment comes from something as dramatic as holding a tank over our head. However, it might seem that way in the moment.

Those four losing-everything-in-life months I experienced changed the trajectory of my life. I still had a war to fight and win, but with chaos reining it was a police officer outside of Memphis that reminded me to slow down. For real.

I was speeding home after rehoming my cats to a friend in Texas since I couldn't take them to a new space with me. I was a mess and a long road trip was a good opportunity to cleanse the emotions and to not be concerned about bothering someone else. Then I was pulled over.

The officer was very kind. I was visibly upset and she asked if there was more going on than just getting pulled over. I quietly said, "Yes," and she told me, "Whatever you're going through won't last. Slow down so you don't miss whatever you need to learn from this experience. You get to choose what to be and what you're going to do from here." Then she handed me my speeding ticket.

Lesson learned. Pay attention.

And, I did. I got home and started becoming more aware of everything about myself and my surroundings. How my actions would affect others. How others' behavior affected me. How I could choose to change an emotional reaction and turn it into a productive force for my clients. How I could use the coaching tools I offered to others on myself on a daily basis to get centered enough to make a plan with a healthy, vibrant vision for my life. How I could choose a support system of friends and colleagues that weren't fakes. I developed a lot of self-awareness and strategy that I didn't have prior to those four months.

This hero's journey can be painful. Getting through the battles and coming to a defining moment is all worth it come victory time.

So, what do you do when faced with your own defining moment?

You dig deep. Take a deep breath. This is where you put all you've learned about yourself, from your mentor, with your team - everything you've got - and take that step forward toward the enemy. Toward the thing you fear the most. Face it head on and watch it disappear. Move forward.

Yell your battle cry.

And Go!

"I THINK PAIN IS WHAT MAKES YOU A HERO. IT'S LIKE A PRESSURE THAT EITHER FORMS A DIAMOND OR GRINDS YOU INTO DUST. " ~BEAST BOY

P.S. And don't worry, Superman came back to life with the help of his "Superfriends."

 # THE VICTORY

THE AIR IS FILLED WITH A NEWFOUND PEACE. DUST SETTLES OVER THE PILE OF RUBBLE FROM THE CHAOS OF BATTLE. THE ENEMY HAS BEEN DEFEATED. THE HERO IS SCARRED, BUT STANDING, WITH HER OWN THOUGHTS WHILE HER TEAM STABILIZES AND SECURES THE AREA.

THE EMOTIONS AND PHYSICAL EXERTION FROM THE BATTLE HAVE LEFT THEM ALL EXHAUSTED.

THE PEOPLE AROUND THEM SEE ONLY THAT THE ENEMY IS DESTROYED AND START CHEERING.

Chapter 12
Celebration

"WE SHALL CELEBRATE WITH ICE CREAM!"

~Wonder Woman

Standing in the midst of the destruction caused by the battle, the hero stands victorious. The battle is won. Time to recover. Time to sift through the ashes to see what remains. The hero finds that only remnants of his former self survived. He is a new Super being. He is not able to return to the comfort zone he once knew. He is protector of his world. Always vigilant. Always open and willing for a new quest. Always being super. But first, a time to celebrate the moment.

Celebrating a job well done looks different for everyone. For some it might be ticker-tape parades, for others a simple Shawarma meal with friends after saving New York City from an alien invasion.

Remember the example of Johnny George? During my interview with him he shared what the experience was like being in front of that Shark Tank panel of investors, and what happened when he walked the hall behind the set.

"Before going on the show, I just said to myself 'Win or lose it's going to be on national TV!'"

Johnny went on to talk about how he thought of his mentors during the presentation, "I just pretended my dad and grandpa were there with me. We made a simple solution to a very complex problem that would help people. It has always been about helping people and having fun doing what I love."

As he walked the long hall to the wrap-up scene, the stage crew applauded him and gave him lots of "thumbs up." His love for his family and passion to help people resonated with them all. It was heartwarming to Johnny to see and hear that people care.

A time of celebration is an ancient concept. There are holidays, anniversaries, birthdays, memorials, championship games, record-breaking events, and so on. Our friends, family, sidekicks, teammates, and mentors are there to help us celebrate.

Yet, one thing I know is damn near impossible for the business leaders I work with to do is... to take time to celebrate the victories no matter the size. One of the elements I include within a strategic plan is the celebration when certain milestones happen. For example, once this book is in print - I am treating myself to a new Wonder Woman graphic novel for my collection!

Celebrating progress helps to keep you motivated, to keep you going. It's a time of recharge and reflection.

Chapter 13
Reflection

"TRUE HAPPINESS IS FOUND ALONG A MIDDLE ROAD. THERE LIES THE BALANCE AND THE HARMONY - WITH REASON AND EMOTION. NOT AT WAR, BUT HAND IN HAND."

~Aquaman

Once a battle is won, there is always a time of quiet. A time to reflect and look back at all that has taken place throughout the experience. To take a breather and decide what's next.

When you look back on the quest, the battles, the defining moments, you realize you do have a choice in how to create the life you want. You control how you are going to show up in your own adventure of life.

When I became aware of this Being Super concept, I reflected on all that has happened in my life. As I continued the practice of reflecting, I could see the drastic difference in how I approached everything. It's definitely been an adventure, and still is. I continue to lose plenty of battles, I also win plenty of battles, and I continue to bounce back, to get right back up, to fight on.

In the process of writing this book, I have had a tremendous amount of reflection time. It's part of the process that is not to be missed. In sports it would be the "review tape." In the military, an after-action report. In the spy movies, a "debriefing". Reflection gives you the opportunity to take an eagle-eye view of what happened. To see the big picture and watch for the details of what can be done differently if a similar challenge presents itself.

Wonder Woman's place of reflection is on the beaches of Themyscira, where she can reconnect with herself while taking the time to review and recharge.

Superman goes to his Fortress of Solitude.

Spiderman has the tops of skyscrapers.

Captain America has his motorcycle and an open road.

Wolverine has a pool table in the bar.

I have a porch swing and my journal.

Where do you go? How do you reflect on life's adventures?

Chapter 14
Now What?

The hero makes it through the battle victorious, the celebrations are over, cleanup has begun. Now, a new normal sets in.

Knowing he can't go back to the person he was before this experience, there are new habits, new mindsets and training to always be alert to new adventures and be at his best.

And never fear...there's always a new adventure just over the horizon.

 **CONTINUING ADVENTURES**

THE ALARM RINGS. THE VOICE OVER THE AIR TELLS OF A DESPOT TRYING TO TAKE OVER THE WORLD. A SIGNAL SHINES IN THE SKY.

THE HERO DOESN'T WAIVER. HE GOES TO HIS BUNKER, PULLS OUT THE UNIFORM AND TOOLS, NOTIFIES HIS TEAM, AND HEADS OUT TO SAVE THE WORLD, AGAIN.

Chapter 15
Origin Stories, Codes & Creeds

"THEY'RE THE BEST EVER. NOT BECAUSE THEY'RE THE MOST POWERFUL. NOT ALL OF THEM. AND IT'S NOT JUST BECAUSE THEY WERE THE FIRST. IT'S BECAUSE THEY'RE SPECIAL. THEY'VE PROVED IT TIME AND AGAIN. THEY MAKE THE HARD CHOICES, THEY SET THE EXAMPLE. THEY DO WHAT'S RIGHT, NOT WHAT'S EASIEST. AND THEY ALWAYS COME OUT ON TOP."

~Steel to Supergirl in Justice League Unlimited

Your Being Super journey doesn't affect only you. Remember, you have mentors, team members, friends, even fans that notice how you handle all the stages from getting the call of starting a new quest to celebrating victory.

How would you share all that with someone new?

You now have an origin story

The key thing about origin stories is that they don't formulate until the adventure is complete. Otherwise, there wouldn't have been an origin. That's why this subject is toward the end of the book and not the beginning.

Once you have experienced a heroic adventure, you can define where it began. It's a great opportunity to use the reflection time to get really clear about the hero you are and the hero you will continue to grow into. It's your story to share.

When I went through training to become an executive coach, one of our activities was to formulate our victim-to-victory story. That's how the origin story works. It explains where you came from, what you've gone through, and how the experience developed you into who you are now.

Get a journal and start writing it all out. Return to read it in times of struggle.

Share your story with someone who needs to hear how you beat your enemy.

Share how you have developed into someone new.

Share how you have become someone who knows how they want to approach life.

Share how you have become someone with a code you live by.

A Code to live by

"AN AMAZON DOES WHAT IS RIGHT NO MATTER THE COST."
~WONDER WOMAN, BLOOD-LINES

A code to live by is developed by bringing together the core values you defined during the quest and the learning lessons from the battles. It's the mix between what's important to you at your core, and what you won't put up with. It's knowing your philosophy for life and living by it. Your value system and how you will live it out. It's the Truth, Justice, and The American Way sort of thing.

The code concept is not new. In my lifetime, I have been exposed to multiple types of codes from classics like Gene Autrey's Cowboy Code.

1. The Cowboy must never shoot first, hit a smaller man, or take unfair advantage.
2. He must never go back on his word, or a trust confided in him.
3. He must always tell the truth.
4. He must be gentle with children, the elderly, and animals.

5. He must not advocate or possess racially or religiously intolerant ideas.
6. He must help people in distress.
7. He must be a good worker.
8. He must keep himself clean in thought, speech, action, and personal habits.
9. He must respect women, parents, and his nation's laws.
10. The Cowboy is a patriot.

From <http://cowpokeradio.com/gene-autry-cowboy-code/>

... to Gibbs' rules on NCIS.

Rule 1: Never let suspects sit together.
Other Rule 1: Never screw over your partner.
Rule 4: Best way to keep a secret. Keep it to yourself. Second-best, tell one other person—if you must. There is no third best.
Rule 5: You don't waste good.
Rule 6: Never say you're sorry.
Rule 8: Never take anything for granted.
Rule 9: Never go anywhere without a knife.
Rule 15: Always work as a team.

Rule 16: If someone thinks he has the upper hand, break it.

Rule 18: It's better to seek forgiveness than ask permission.

Rule 22: Never, ever bother Gibbs in interrogation.

Rule 23: Never mess with a Marine's coffee if you want to live.

Rule 28: When you need help, ask.

Rule 36: If it feels like you're being played, you probably are.

Rule 38: Your case, your lead.

Rule 39: There is no such thing as a coincidence.

Rule 40: If it seems like someone's out to get you, they are.

Rule 42: Never accept an apology from somebody who just sucker-punched you.

Rule 44: First things first, hide the women and children.

Rule 51: Sometimes you're wrong.

From <https://www.cheatsheet.com/entertainment/ncis-gibbs-rules.html/>

Gibbs has a lot of rules to live by, I just listed my favorites.

Codes provide an ethical structure. Having the code gives you the boundaries to live within. The code sets the non-negotiables, what you will and won't do. The code sets the priorities.

A code is a system.

A creed takes it one step further into written vision, almost manifesto style that tells the world what you believe about your code.

> *"My people have a saying, 'Don't kill if you can wound, don't wound if you can subdue, don't subdue if you can pacify, and don't raise your hand at all until you have first extended it.'"*
>
> ~Wonder Woman

Remember the Bikers Against Child Abuse? They have a creed they share so people understand the significance behind their mission.

B.A.C.A. Creed
Adapted from "The Fellowship of the Unashamed"

I am a Member of Bikers Against Child Abuse. The die has been cast. The decision has been made. I have stepped over the line. I won't look back, let up, slow down, back away, or be still.

My past has prepared me, my present makes sense, and my future is secure. I'm finished and done with low living, sight walking, small planning, smooth knees, colorless dreams, tamed visions, mundane talking, cheap giving, and dwarfed goals.

I no longer need pre-eminence, prosperity, position, promotions, plaudits, or popularity. I don't have to be right, first, tops, recognized, praised, regarded, or rewarded. I now live by the faith in my works, and lean on the strength of my brothers and sisters. I love with patience, live by prayer, and labor with power.

My fate is set, my gait is fast, my goal is the ultimate safety of children. My road is narrow, my way is rough, my companions are tried and true, my Guide is reliable, my mission is clear. I cannot be bought, compromised, detoured, lured away, turned back, deluded, or delayed. I will not flinch in the face of sacrifice, hesitate in the presence of adversity, negotiate at the table of the enemy, ponder at the pool of popularity, or meander in the maze of mediocrity.

I won't give up, shut up, let up, until I have stayed up, stored up, prayed up, paid up, and showed up for all wounded children. I must go until I drop, ride until I give out, and work till He stops me. And when He comes for His own, He will have no problem recognizing me, for He will see my B.A.C.A. backpatch and know that I am one of His. I am a Member of Bikers Against Child Abuse, and this is my creed.

Founder of Bikers Against Child Abuse, Inc.

From <*https://bacaworld.org/mission/*>

How to put this concept to use in your own life?

Write it out.

Revise after reflecting on each new adventure.

Repeat.

Keep a journal and write in it daily. From that journal you will find your code. Then post your code and creed on the wall, in a place you will see it every day. You will find that over time you will make additions and revisions based on what you experience during new quests and battles. Keep it in front of you, with you on your phone, in your wallet, your planner, post-its in the bathroom, until it sinks in and is instilled in your everyday life.

Chapter 16
Stay in Training

"I HAVE MUCH TO LEARN. I KNOW THAT NOW."

~Thor

The Watchtower is more than a satellite in space for the Justice League, monitoring the stars for new invasions, it's also a training center. Even superheroes need to "use it or lose it."

To be successful at what we want to accomplish, we have to keep moving forward. That includes staying in training to keep our edge, to learn new things, to level-up. The training enables us to increase our stamina, be stronger, faster, better than what we were before. It sharpens our strengths and helps us deal with our weaknesses that came to light during regrouping after a battle.

Consistent training is important for more than just sports: playing a musical instrument, singing, farming, auto mechanic-ing, leading a team, running a business, parenting, marriage, and so much more!

Continuing to learn and grow empowers us to **expand our comfort zones on purpose**.

I work in the field of training and development. I started studying success principles and habits in high school. It still amazes me how impactful it can be when someone goes through a training on a new skill, or even to learn something new about what they already thought they knew everything about. They come away more confident and ready to take on new challenges.

Training can be a release for pent up stress. Training can be a recharge of internal batteries.

Training is rarely done alone. Your team is there to help keep you in shape. To keep you accountable. To even gift you with new tech to upgrade your skills, like Spiderman's iron suit after helping defeat Thanos with all the other Marvel heroes.

Set the environment

Avengers have a training room, X-men have the danger room, Justice League has a training room.

I have Disney World.

I have small notebooks on hand and do my training and strategic planning while waiting in lines. I even have a whole 3-day experience for business owners to do the same as a group.

When I can get a client convinced to get out of their normal environment into a more creative space, I know their team is going to experience something they'll never forget. And, they will want to retain and use all they learn.

What space inspires you? The gym? The stage? A beach? A racecar garage? An amusement park? A bench under a tree?

Find a good spot that inspires you. Take your training with you (your coach, online courses, books, etc.). Make it a full experience.

Keep training - especially in the areas which makes you the most uncomfortable.

I still giggle each time I see Wonder Woman in a training moment of her biggest challenge - conversations with her mother. She practices over and over what she will say to prepare for what the Queen, the woman she respects the most, will say and do.

Training is important in all the moments in your life. What is an area you could be getting training in now?

Chapter 17
Meanwhile...

"THE REAL TEST OF HONOR ISN'T IN HOW YOU DIE. IT'S IN HOW YOU LIVE."

~Superman to Draga
(episode of The Justice League animation 'War World')

In every story there are other events going on around the main scene. Movies like the Avengers bring a team together to share the storyline, with each individual knowing that their role plays to their strengths. Black Widow is not going to "Hulk" out or cast sorcery from her hands. When one of the Avengers is singled out for their own movie storyline, guest appearances by the other Avengers are always in a supporting role.

Sometimes WE are the supporting role. Everyone has something going on. Everywhere. All. The. Time.

Even after what felt like the biggest adventure the hero had ever experienced, another adventure waits around the corner. That's why there are multiple movies, more comics, more books, an ever-evolving heroic character universe. Multiple universes. The Multiverse.

Remember, you and other heroes around you, are either going into a battle, exiting a battle, or are in one right now. Our stories intertwine into adventures of epic proportions at times.

Be willing to be someone else's supporting role while they go on their own quest.

Chapter 18
The Continuing Adventures

"DUDE, CAPTAIN AMERICA NEEDS MY HELP. THERE'S NO BETTER REASON TO GET BACK IN."
~Sam Wilson, Captain America Winter Soldier

I have more than one shelf full of Wonder Woman stories. 75 years of stories. One right after another. More quests, more self-discovering, new weapons and costumes, more team-ups, a LOT more battles, and definitely more victories. Continuing adventures will happen as long as there are writers to create and people to read or watch the story.

Do you know how many superhero stories there are? There are literally thousands from multiple companies with hundreds of writers and artists bringing characters to life with different personalities, strengths, origin stories and adventures.

There is one very unique character in all the "universes:" Donna Troy. Through the years, writers have taken Donna on vastly different twists and turns:

- She was a younger version of Wonder Woman who goes on to fight with the Teen Titans in the 70s.
- In a 1980s revival, Donna was an orphaned child found in the remains of a fire, only to be put up for adoption by her adoptive parent who couldn't take care of her. Winding up in a child-selling ring,

superheroes save her and bring her in as one of their own.

- After most of DC's hero stories were rewritten, Donna's story became one of myth as the Titan, Rhea, saved young Donna from a fire. Raised on New Cronus (a different planet), Donna takes on a new moniker, Troia, and takes on a new costume incorporating gifts from the Titans of myth.
- In the 1990s, Donna was re-written again, this time as a magical duplicate of a young Princess Diana (Wonder Woman). Thinking the girl was Diana, the villain Dark Angel kidnapped Donna and cursed her to live her life as an endless stream of reinvented scenarios that would begin again at the lowest points.
- As the DC series, Infinite Crisis, was released, Donna was written as a merger of all the versions of Donna Troy within the multiverse and given the responsibility of watching over the chronicles of all the universes.
- For a time, Donna took on the mantle of Wonder Woman after Diana stepped down because of her own crisis.
- In the "Rebirth" season of DC writing, Donna was created as an Amazon by a sorceress to usurp Diana's claim to the throne. Donna was defeated and went on her own soul-searching journey to later become Fate.

Yes, Zeus chooses Donna to replace the three witches of mythological fate.

To say this character has had complications is an understatement. She has had numerous reinventions, lots of adversity, and amazing adventures on her own and with her teams.

Like Donna, you have also experienced many iterations and adversity in life. On your own, with your family, and with your teams. There are times you get to decide your own twist of fate, and other times fate deals you a different card to play.

My friend Diana is a great example. She is one of the strongest, funniest, most resilient people I know. She has gone through more than a "second act" with her life:

- Started out of college with an Associate Degree in computer programming
- Got married and had kids, thinking she would be a stay-at-home mom
- Started a job in singing telegrams that evolved into event planning
- Started a business on her own as a balloon designer for events
- Brought in the whole family to work with her, including the grandkids, to evolve the

business into a special event production company
- Husband had a stroke and survived, with complications, for over 20 years
- Business was on the brink of bankruptcy when, after some prayer time with her pastor friend, a big job designing and producing floating icebergs for Coors fell in her lap that propelled her company onto the national scene
- Purchased another business to have it dissolved in a lawsuit with the previous owners
- Her husband recently passed away and, in the process, she became an advocate for those dealing with nursing home and Medicare issues
- She has plans for even bigger things as she recently celebrated "leveling up" to 70 years of age.

Throughout each twist and turn, Diana has kept her faith and her resolve to win the fight, no matter how chaotic she feels in the midst of it all.

Have you heard of Caleb from the Bible? Caleb was part of the tribe of Judah in the Old Testament. When Moses was alive and led the Israelites out of the wilderness, he sent a group of spies to the land across the Jordan. Caleb was 40 years old during that mission. Fast forward another 45 years, and Caleb goes to Moses' successor, Joshua, and says, "As yet I am as strong this day as on the day that Moses sent me; just as my strength was then, so now is my strength for war...Now, therefore, give me this mountain of which the Lord spoke in that day..." (Joshua 14:11,12)

This dude was 85 years old and ready to conquer a mountain as his own! I don't know about you, but I think the only mountain I want to climb when I'm 85 is the one attached to the water slide on my very own pool.

Caleb may fit under the Epic Hero classification.

Regardless of the type of hero you are, you have a choice with this life you've been given. Will you let the circumstances of events happen to you, or will you step up into the adventure to be the hero you know you are? Or even be the hero you know you've always been.

There was a video that was being shared recently, of an elderly gentleman being pushed around a parking lot in his wheelchair. What makes this video so spectacular is that the parking lot wasn't just a parking lot, nor was the man just elderly. He was a former stuntman, wearing a cape, getting a running push by an attendant over the ramps set up around the lot.

The utter joy on both their faces made me cheer through my own tears of joy watching it all happen.

And then there's Bob. Bob was featured on a Hershey's chocolate commercial. He walks to the store and buys big Hershey's chocolate bars and hands them out to people every day. He does it to bring joy. Bob is 94!

Mary Kay Ash was over 45 years old when she opened her first storefront selling beauty products. A business that would continue to grow into a multi-billion dollar company.

Colonel Sanders was 65 when he started Kentucky Fried Chicken.

Jack Canfield was 48 years old when he teamed up with Mark Victor Hansen to create the book, Chicken Soup for the Soul.

Susan Boyle, the shy, devout 48-year-old stepped onto the stage for an audition on Britain's Got Talent.

Walt Disney was 54 years old when Disneyland opened.

Even Tootsie's Orchid Lounge in Nashville wouldn't have nurtured hundreds of country music stars over the years if it hadn't been for Hattie Louise Bess, aka Tootsie Bess. Bess was almost 60 years old when she bought the little bar, Mom's, that backed up via an alley to the Ryman in downtown Nashville, Tennessee, and renamed it. Her passion for aspiring artists helped the city become a vibrant music scene. She was rumored to have slipped $5 or $10 to down-on-their-luck musicians and singers to keep them going. Her personal effort helped early artists like Kris Kristofferson, Willie Nelson, Roger Miller, Waylon Jennings, Patsy Cline, Dolly Parton and many more go on to stardom. Almost every artist that comes to town performs at Tootsie's sometime in their career: Garth Brooks, Keith Urban, Trisha Yearwood, Taylor Swift, and even Aerosmith.

You're never too young, or too old, to start a new adventure.

"FURY ALWAYS SAID, 'A MAN CAN ACCOMPLISH ANYTHING WHEN HE REALIZES HE'S A PART OF SOMETHING BIGGER. A TEAM OF PEOPLE WHO CAN SHARE THAT CONVICTION CAN CHANGE THE WORLD.' SO WHAT DO YOU SAY? YOU READY TO CHANGE THE WORLD?"
~AGENT COULSON ON AGENTS OF S.H.I.E.L.D.

Remember...

"A hero is someone who is concerned about other people's well-being, and will go out of his or her way to help them even if there is no chance of a reward."
~Stan Lee

The creators of superheroes; Jerry Seigel with Joe Shuster (Superman), Bob Kane with Bill Finger (Batman), William Moulton Marston (Wonder Woman), Jack Kirby with Joe Simon (Captain America), and most famously Stan Lee with Jack Kirby (X-Men, Spiderman, the Incredible Hulk, Avengers, and more), are imperfect people who understood that readers need hope and inspiration in times of trouble. The Being Super life adventure concept is something they incorporate over and over in the storylines, with the colorful heroes fighting world-threatening bad guys while dealing with feelings every human has of not measuring up to other people's standards, of not measuring up to perceived expectations.

The inspiration for these super powered heroes comes from normal, everyday people like yourself who stepped into moments as if they were wearing a cape and yelling, *"EXCELSIOR!"*

My hope, now, is that you have been able to look at your own life and see your hero story unfold. How you were called to a quest. All that you discovered about yourself during the quest. How you sharpened your skills in battle. Note the moment that helped define "you" as you came face-to-face with your villain.

And celebrate. Celebrate all that you have accomplished. Celebrate all you that you have. Celebrate that you have a new opportunity every day for a new epic journey.

Being Super is not a part-time adventure. It's a full-time lifestyle.

Go. Be Super.

Christy Smallwood is the Chief Strategic Guide and founder of Eagle Eye Strategies. She helps people solve problems strategically to maximize time, effort, and money. Her background includes 20+ years in media, marketing and advertising, consumer behavior, leadership design, executive business coaching, and professional training.

Christy's mission is to break the status quo of small business, bring order to chaos clearing the clutter of stinking thinking, spark the inspiration of big ideas and audacious goals for purpose-driven entrepreneurs and light a fire under their asses to bring it all to life.

Being Super is available for more than your reading pleasure. Christy has used Being Super for workshops, strategic planning sessions, and keynote messages. Want to bring Being Super to your group? Message Christy@EagleEyeStrategies.biz for info.

To learn more about Christy visit www.ChristySmallwood.com.

www.ingramcontent.com/pod-product-compliance
Lightning Source LLC
Chambersburg PA
CBHW060117260626
47160CB00005B/1918